A Year Behind Bars

*When you have lost your inns, you may drown your empty selves,
for you will have lost the heart of England.*

Hilaire Belloc

A Year Behind Bars

Published by
La Puce Publications
87 Laburnum Grove
North End
Portsmouth PO2 0HG

Telephone: 023 92 678148
Facsimile: 023 92 665070

This paperback edition 2001

ISBN 0 9523635 5 0

Designed and typeset by Nigel at Christianson Hoper Norman
Reprographics by SP Digital
Printed in Great Britain by Borcombe Printers PLC, Hampshire

There are said to be more than 80,000 public houses in Britain. According to official statistics, someone visits a British pub every three seconds. That someone is not always George East, though he claims to be doing his best to keep up with the average.

A committed pubologist, George has been writing about inns, taverns, hostelries, good old-fashioned boozers and the people who run and use them for more than twenty years. In *A Year Behind Bars*, the author invites us to join a new publican as he attempts to create the perfect local...and discovers that life on the other side of the bar counter is not always plain sailing.

All the characters in this book are by necessity fictitious, but anyone who has ever run or regularly used a pub will instantly recognise most of them. If you enjoy visiting the Great British Pub you'll love this revealing diary of a year behind bars. If you have ever thought about the delights of running your own pub, perhaps it might be better to read no further.

Other books by George East include:

Home & Dry in France
René & Me
French Letters
French Flea Bites

Author's disclaimer

All the stories in this book are untrue and all the characters fictitious and should not be taken to bear any semblance to any persons living, dead or permanently pissed. All the names, locations and situations were invented to avoid possible embarrassment, legal action or grievous bodily harm.

A Brief History of the British Public House

The origins of the Great British Pub are understandably lost in the mists of time and alcoholic haze. However, some eminent pubologists believe that the tradition of inviting people into your front room for a drink and then charging them for the pleasure must have begun in Scotland.

Others claim our great gift to the world originated when an entrepreneurial Ancient Briton saw a chance to take revenge on the Roman occupiers. Virtually overnight, the story goes, the first pubs appeared at all garrison gates, offering the inmates a taste of British culture and hospitality and unlimited access to the national beverage. Lacking the climatic conditions or inclination to make wine, the first British innkeeper allegedly invented and served his overseas customers with a drink made from fermenting (ie rotting) vegetables laced with honey. For marketing purposes, this concoction was advertised as the nectar of the British gods. To the locals, it was known as Arghh, the Celtic deity of bodily functions.

Over the centuries and in the way of all living languages, the word evolved to Ale. Some historians claim that the quality of our national drink accounts for the sudden and final departure of the Roman legions, and is also the reason why British beer was for so long held in such low esteem by other foreign visitors.

Though there is little hard evidence for the above account of the origins of the British pub, much excitement was caused by the recent discovery of some unique artefacts uncovered at a dig on the site of a Roman encampment near Colchester.

Along with a board bearing the traces of a sign showing a busty and alluring Celtic barmaid and a legionnaire's helmet, they also found what may be one of the first ever pub notices. When translated from ancient Latin and allowing for contemporary vocabulary and common usage, the sign read:

Please do not ask the guv'nor for credit, as a punch in the mouth often offends.

Little is known about the public house in medieval times, but the enormous growth in popularity of going down the pub and drinking vast amounts of beer to forget one's troubles during these hard times is said to be why the period is known to historians as the Dark Ages.

Moving on to the 16th century, a survey in 1557 confirmed that there were up to 25,000 public houses in England. As the population was then less than four million, we were obviously developing a taste for our traditional home-from-home.

By 1725, a census revealed that 'stronge drynk' was on sale from more than 6,000 homes and shops in Greater London, which meant that there were, on paper, more pubs than houses, a tradition which continues to this day in some parts of the capital.

The situation was made even worse (or better, depending upon your view) when the Beerhouse Act of 1830 allowed any ratepayer to turn his house into a pub. As there were nearly as many public houses as customers to use them, the major brewers fought back by building huge 'gin palaces' to persuade drinkers to go out rather than stay in for a drink.

At the start of World War I (1914-18), there were around 90,000 registered public houses in Britain, and licensing hours were introduced to prevent munitions factory workers from staggering back to work in the afternoon and blowing up the neighbourhood.

By the late 1980s, somebody in authority had realised that the Great War was over, and all-day drinking was once again permitted. But the damage was done, and the great British public had got into the habit of spending at least part of the working day sober.

Though nobody has apparently bothered to count and catalogue them all, there are nowadays believed to be around 80,000 proper public houses in Britain, all with their individual ambience, character and charm. Regardless of the inevitable march of so-called progress, the true character of the Great British Pub has changed little over the centuries, and is still an institution admired and even envied throughout the civilised world. If not always by individual customers.

for PJS, without whom AYBB
would not have happened

DECEMBER

My wife has bought me a pub for Christmas. Or rather, she has allowed me to buy one for myself. Soon, I will be able to drink at cost price and entertain hundreds of customers and friends in my front room. What's more, I will actually be paid for enjoying myself instead of shelling out to visit other people's pubs.

I am also a man with a mission, which is to create the perfect public house. In doing so, I shall be following in the footsteps of John Fothergill, author of *An Innkeeper's Diary*. Like me, he was a man of letters and familiar with the celebrities of the day. From the 1920s, the Spread Eagle at Oxford became a popular watering-hole for such artists and writers as Augustus John, George Bernard Shaw and Evelyn Waugh. Literary hangers-on like the Sitwells were also regulars in his snug bar.

In this age of plastic pubs, I shall concentrate on offering the traditional delights of the classic local to ordinary people. Like the landord of the Spread Eagle, I will keep a record of my progress, but I shall not start my first year behind bars with his attitude. He established an almost breathtaking reputation for rudeness during his time as a licensee, and died in straitened circumstances after half a lifetime in the business.

Perhaps he was not a natural innkeeper. It may be that he had a darker view of human nature than me. I like to think that I can bring out the best in people in any circumstances, and innkeeping is in my blood. My grandfather ran a corner local in this city more than sixty years ago, and I have visited and spent more time in pubs than most people I know.

The only cloud on my horizon is my wife's reservations about the new project. When I initially suggested the idea she was unusually pessimistic about our chances of finding happiness behind bars. She forecast that running a pub would be absolutely nothing like visiting one, and that my favourite hobby would become much less appealing when I had to do it for a living. She even predicted I would drink more than ever, put on masses of weight, become coarsened by exposure to the true state of human nature, and that it would all end in tears. It is unusual for her to take such a cynical view of my ideas, and she has always been supportive of whatever trail I have chosen to follow across the years. Admittedly, she prefers animals to people and has a low estimation of human nature, but I am sure she will come round when she sees how successful I am. After much debate, she has at least agreed to give me a year to prove that I can make my dream a reality, and after months of searching for just the right pub, I have found it in the Ship Leopard Tavern.

It is true that the Leo is in the inner city, and does not have a lot of natural appeal in its architecture and setting. Built around the turn of the century, it is a fairly typical and undistinguished corner local. There are some fine examples of decorative etching on the windows which have not been broken over the years, but the glazed green tiles covering the brickwork make it look, according to my wife, more like a public lavatory than a public house. Inside, it is sad to see how changing tastes have vandalised what must have been a classic example of an Edwardian local. There are still some echoes of past elegance and solidity, but now laminated plastic has triumphed over lovingly carved hardwood, and harsh neon strip lighting has replaced the gently glowing gas mantles. Apart from The Ship Leopard, there are another eight pubs in the close proximity, but as I said to my wife, this is a good sign. So many pubs crowded together in such a small area must mean that there is a demand for their services. Besides, having visited and spied on the opposition, I do not expect much serious competition.

Apart from my ideas for luring customers away from the other pubs on the strip, I have already started work on a business plan and phased strategy, with monthly budgets, turnover targets and key objectives. The man from the brewery company which owns the Ship Leopard is nearly as enthusiastic as me, and confided how pleased he was to have found someone with such an obvious flair for the business. With my mix of acumen and natural ability, he says he is sure we will be a great success in our new venture.

We do not take over until next month, which is a disappointment but probably for the best. The outgoing landlord advised us to leave all the complications and aggravations of the Christmas trading period to him. We will make our seamless transition during a time when things begin to quieten down. He is clearly a considerate man, but obviously not cut out for the job. I have noticed that he does not go out of his way to entertain the regulars beyond a grunt when he serves them, and his customer service techniques seem virtually non-existent. I don't wish to belittle his efforts over the past decade at the Leo, but he is clearly not suited to the role. He has even cautioned me about the customers 'taking liberties' and how important it is not to give credit to or trust anyone, including the staff. He is also, I have noticed, nothing short of penny-pinching. Something in his past has soured him, or perhaps he is just not made of the right stuff to be a successful innkeeper.

I will obviously have much to learn in my new life, but cannot see the difference between running a pub and any other business involving people. My wife is still full of dark foreboding, but has agreed to give me a chance to show what I can do. If for some reason things do not work out, we can easily sell up and at an increased price given that I will have doubled or even quadrupled the takings.

Whatever happens, it is sure to be a memorable year.

Pubs with no Beer

On Christmas Eve, 1867, the first British Working Man's Public House was opened to great acclaim from the various temperance organisations. The unique selling-point was that this prototype of a proposed nationwide chain sold no alcoholic beverage, and the snappy advertising slogan read:

A Public House Without The Drink
Where Men May Read And Smoke And Think
Then Sober Home Return
A Stepping Stone This House You'll Find
Come Leave Your Rum And Beer Behind
And Other Pleasures Learn...

Somewhat predictably, this desperate attempt to stop the lower orders enjoying themselves was a total failure, and the first dry pub closed through lack of support within a year of opening...

JANUARY

Running a pub may not be as easy as I thought.

When I told my father that I was becoming part of a great British institution, he asked me why I would want to live in an institution. He recalled his father (who was also a licensee) saying the only thing wrong with the pub business was the customers, and I am beginning to see what grandfather meant. My wife has also been a little tight-lipped since our arrival, and has started referring to the Ship Leopard as The Lubyanka or even The Loonybin. When I asked her to explain, she said that she doesn't relish the idea of living in a prison for a year, especially as all the inmates are clearly certifiable. I pointed out that we have inherited the trade, and that it is accepted in the industry that the customers reflect the character of the landlord. She would soon see some changes when I started to attract my sort of people. At this, she gave a hollow laugh and said it might then be an idea to go the whole hog and put bars on the windows and issue the staff with white coats.

Thursday 7th

I am going to start a register of weird visitors. Most of the regular customers are not what I would call normal. Some seem to be from another planet. I have always prided myself in an understanding of human nature, and bought a book on psychology last month to help with the study and treatment of my regulars. Given the behaviour of some of them, I should have bought a book on psychiatry. The latest refugee from *The Twilight Zone* arrived this morning and calmly introduced himself as the original Baron Von Richthofen. According to the locals, he is a wealthy scrap metal dealer who lives in a rambling, near-derelict house in the poshest part of the city. He is understandably unpopular with the neighbours as he likes to take his work home with him, and his back garden is full of old cookers and the odd government surplus tank. When he shambled in, I had my doubts about serving him as he looked like a vagrant, but he pulled out a twenty pound note and ordered a large schnapps, so immediately became a valued client. As the bar was deserted, we fell into conversation and he told me quite matter-of-factly that he was a reincarnation of the illustrious Red Baron. He said he can clearly remember every one of his dog-fights with British air aces as well as the exact moment and circumstances of his heroic death. When he had spent all his money, I escorted him to the door in case he had trouble finding it, and was quite disappointed not to find a World War I bi-plane parked at the kerb. After giving me a crisp military salute, he pulled on a flying helmet and goggles and buzzed away in a battered old sports car while singing a German marching song.

Later, I learned that the car is a very rare 1950's Ferrari, and worth at least twice as much as the freehold of the Ship Leopard.

Wednesday 13th

It is after midnight, and I am sitting alone in the lounge bar. There is a peculiar stillness about any place which has once been full of life, but my problem at the moment is the silence in the Leo during opening hours. Takings are not nearly as good as I had been led to expect from the departing licensee, but it is after all the month after Christmas. Perhaps my predecessor has taken most of his regular patrons with him to his new pub, though a customer said yesterday that the Leo is actually doing better business than usual at this time of year. He also took delight in telling me we are having what is known in the trade as our 'honeymoon', and that the local pubgoers are taking a look at us, and will not be back. He seemed to like the idea of having the place to himself, and passing on bad news is obviously what keeps him happy. Apart from being a Job's comforter, I have already classified him as a self-appointed pub pundit, and there seem to be many of those at the Leo. In my short time as a licensee, I have already found that there is nothing more irritating than people who have never been on the business side of the bar telling you how your pub should be run. Especially when trade is so slack. Another pub truism I have discovered is that every customer thinks he could run any pub better than the present licensee. I am already beginning to see why the previous landlord at the Leo found it difficult to look pleased when some of his regulars arrived to tell him what he was doing wrong.

Thursday 14th

Tonight was comparatively brisk in the public bar. It was a darts night, which increased the usual number of customers. I have been keeping a head count, and it was the first time since our free opening party that we reached double figures, not including myself and the staff. All went reasonably well for our first attempt at entertaining a visiting team, except for the sandwiches. As our captain explained, there is an ongoing competition between participating pubs to have the biggest and best spread of food for visiting players (for which the home team pays), and our team were very disappointed with the two plates of paste sandwiches that my wife grudgingly served up. Normally, the teams would expect much more of a variety and choice, with pickled onions, roast potatoes and even pig's trotters as accessories. The match (which we lost) went reasonably well except for an incident when the visiting team complained that the light over the board was not at the exact angle, height and brightness demanded by league regulations. The shade is also peppered with holes caused by the ladies darts team, and the visitors said this lessened the brilliance of the light and caused them to miss many vital shots. From my observations, it seems that the more mediocre the ability of an individual player or team, the more they will blame the environment and equipment for lack of success. I tried to lighten the atmosphere by buying the players a drink and letting the visiting landlord beat me in the last game, but they still went off in a surly frame of mind. Totting up the takings after midnight and allowing for the staff, rent, heat light and other expenses it appears we only lost around £100 on the day, so things are getting better.

Looking at the scraps of paper put in the cash register by the staff when I stood a drink, it also seemed that I was the biggest spender of the evening. I don't remember buying half the rounds put down to me, so must organise a more efficient system. It is so easy to hand out courtesy drinks without ringing them up, and I don't want the bar staff getting into bad habits. The outgoing landlord gave me little advice, but he did mutter cryptically that I should 'watch the till', and I can now see what he meant. On my first session with Twiggy our busty barmaid, she insisted on buying me a drink which she made up from the most expensive bottles on the top shelf. It was called a harlot's fart, and I should imagine the flavour was not far away from the real thing. I also noticed she did not put any money in the till for the drink she stood me, nor the one she had herself to join in the celebration.

*   *   *   *   *

I am still full of enthusiasm, but now realise that life on this side of the bar will be very different, and that my estimate for our first month's turnover will be much lower than I had hoped. I did my initial calculations after spending Christmas on a customer-only basis at the Leo, and I was amazed at the money cascading over the bar. Everybody seemed to be enjoying themselves and spending without reserve. At one time I heard the landlord make an aside to Twiggy that they would have to get a bucket of water to throw over the cash register to cool it down, and it was the only time during our many visits that he made a joke or seemed to be remotely happy. For a man with as much personality as a pump handle, he seemed to come alive as the crush grew, and I even caught him smiling at his customers on several occasions.

Now we are in the depths of January, and I did not think that business could be this bad. A new customer is a talking point and the only people coming in are the diehard regulars, who are not the sort of people I had in mind when I planned my creation of the perfect pub. Fothergill says that atmosphere in an inn is created solely by people. If that's true, I think my father's crack about living in an institution may not be so far away from the truth.

Before we took over at the Leo, a friend who used to run a pub said the licensee's main problem is that he can choose his friends but not his customers. After my short time behind bars, it seems to me that the acid test of suitability is to ask yourself if you would have a customer as a guest in your house. So far, the answer is invariably no. The problem at the moment is not being able to do much about the sort of customers I encourage as there are so few to choose from. I can bar the most objectionable types, or be so rude as to make them look elsewhere for a local, but if I only have the sort of people I like on the premises, I will soon be talking to myself.

I suppose I will have to learn to be more tolerant, but we seem to have inherited a collection of individuals who would try the patience of a saint. Some are petty, others merely boring, and some so shallow that, as my Irish granny used to say, you wouldn't be able to see them if they turned sideways. Others could obviously start a row in an empty room, and they all seem to be totally selfish in their view of what a pub is for and why they are using mine. As a result, I am beginning to revise my opinion of the average landlord. I used to believe the wrong sort of people took on the role, but now I can see that they often look so miserable because of the people they have to deal with.

Saturday 16th

Our first fight, but the only severe damage has been to the pub's reputation. During his first official visit last week, I was warned by the local beat bobby to be careful about allowing too many Irish casual workers into the public bar at the same time.

Of Irish descent myself I was shocked at this apparent display of prejudice, and sarcastically asked him if there was a quota agreement amongst the local landlords. He looked at me blankly for a moment, then explained that a large number of itinerant Irish labourers live in a hostel in the area, and drink as hard as they work. They collect their wages on a Saturday morning and do their best to spend them before closing time that evening. Sometimes and especially to an inexperienced landlord, they could be a bit of a handful. I assured him that I would do my best not to encourage them to use the Leo, and immediately made up some posters and leaflets announcing a dress rehearsal for St Patrick's Day. As an extra gimmick, I added a note that glasses of stout would be on sale at half price for anyone with a true Irish accent. Having bribed our paper boy to distribute the handbills around the area, and particularly to the hostel, I spent this morning dressing the public bar with huge paper shamrocks and green bunting, filled the juke box with suitable music, and stood by to see how our first promotion would fare.

By seven o' clock, the Leo was packed with happy men in black suits with muddy trouser bottoms, and the public bar was busier than during the peak Christmas trading hours. It was a joy to see the staff struggling to cope, and I took great pleasure in telling Twiggy to stand by with a bucket of water for the till.

At nine 'o' clock, I considered putting a 'house full' notice on the outer door, but could not bring myself to turn custom away.

The trouble broke out just before closing time, when I light-heartedly challenged a very big man's accent before agreeing to the half-price stout offer. When he said that he came from Belfast, I could not resist querying if that qualified as part of real Ireland, and immediately wished I hadn't. A debate then ensued between customers from both sides of the border about what constituted a proper Irish accent, and words suddenly turned to blows.

An hour later and the public bar was as empty as usual, and I had received an official warning from the police. I spent another hour clearing up the mess while revising my plans for a really lively St Patrick's Day promotion.

Thursday 21st

Although it's my birthday, it has not been as enjoyable as last year, when we spent the day visiting pubs rather than running one. Things started badly when the draymen arrived before dawn had broken across the rooftops, and woke me by making a lot of noise in the road outside. Leaning out of the bedroom window, I observed quite reasonably that I had not finished work till midnight and that, unlike draymen, landlords usually have to go to bed and get up to start work on the same day. The driver showed little sympathy and said he would be happy to work night and day for the money I was earning, and that it didn't rain inside pubs, as far as he knew. He also made a coarse remark about kicking the barmaid out of bed earlier so that I could get some sleep. From my position it was not easy to enter into a philosophical discussion about relative income and responsibility rates, so I told them they would have to come back later. The spokesman for the duo retorted that they had already unloaded and were on their way to the next call, and if I didn't want the stuff, he was sure that passers-by would. Doors and windows in the side street alongside the Leo were already beginning to open, so I had to give in and go down to let the delivery men in.

They may have won the argument, but I got my own back by insisting that they took away all the empties from the former landlord's Christmas bonanza. I also turned down their offer of a bargain tub of bitter that had somehow been loaded on their wagon by mistake. Nor did I give them a tip. Eventually, they departed in a flurry of expletives, leaving broken glass all over the yard, and one of the gates hanging off its hinges. I shall have to talk to the brewery about their customer care training standards.

Friday 22nd

Another poor session, but I have found that there are some

19

consolations for spending endless hours with little to do but look at the door in hope. As far as I know, there are no post-graduate courses which involve studying public houses and what goes on in them, but I can think of no better place for observing human nature in all its diversity. Today, the subject for my consideration has been the traditional pub activity of buying by round.

In theory, it should be all very simple, and merely involve each person in a group taking it in turns to pay for the drinks. In practice, it is a far from straightforward arrangement. In my short time on this side of the bar, I have learned much about how devious some people can be when it comes to not paying their turn.

A typical ploy for the classic round-dodger is to make straight for the toilet when arriving with a group, then answer an alleged call of nature every time glasses in his circle become dangerously low. I have seen some really audacious offenders visit the Gents on a dozen occasions, then seek sympathy for their imaginary prostate condition.

Another favoured device is to pretend to spot a long-lost friend elsewhere in the pub at the vital moment. I have even known advanced round-dodgers arrange for a friend to call on their mobile phones at regular intervals, so they can excuse themselves to go outside to get a better signal just before their turn to be 'in the chair' comes round. By careful manipulation and only paying for a round late on in the session, the skilled operator can also maximise the total number of drinks bought by other people in the circle, then make good his escape before his turn comes round again. With really good timing, he can blame me for not being able to stand his final round before the bell sounds at closing time.

Another common type of freeloader is the stalker, who will literally do the rounds of all suitable groups in the pub, weighing up the prospects and always on the lookout for suitable victims. Like a tiger watching a gathering of antelope at a watering hole, he will wait for exactly the right moment, then strike. As glasses are drained, he will invent a reason for talking to any member of the group he can get away with pretending to know, and the person in the chair will have no option but to include him in the forthcoming round. After claiming his drink, the stalker will find an excuse to move on and wait to strike again.

Some round-dodgers hunt exclusively in pairs, with the male and his female partner looking for any solo drinker they can find a slim excuse to join. Despite all talk of equal rights and responsibilities in the outside world, women in men's company never seem to buy a drink, especially in the Leo. Thus, the solo drinker will be buying two drinks for every one he will receive from the couple. With the more brazen operators of this scam, the female will not have a drink when her partner is buying, but make up for it by graciously agreeing to accept a large one when the unaccompanied man is paying.

According to a book on pub running I bought before taking over at the Leo, the system of taking it in turns to buy a round of drinks should be encouraged by the licensee, as it 'draws people together and encourages social intercourse and conviviality.' As far as I can see, the majority of my younger customers would be much better off following the example of our veterans and buying their own. In the Leo, it is an accepted fact that all single men of retirement age and past sexual activity treat nobody but themselves, though it is rumoured that one of our most unsociable and penny-pinching aged regulars bought Twiggy Bristols a drink last month. When she recovered sufficiently to ask what he was celebrating, he explained that it was the tenth anniversary of his wife's death.

Saturday 23rd

It looks as if I shall have a valuable ally in learning the tricks of the trade. This morning I received an official visit from an interesting character who has run pubs in the city all his life. Tez Eldon is also local president of the Licensed Victuallers Association, and called in to sign me up as a member. He is a real character, and of all the licensees I have met across the years, Tez The Prez is exactly my idea of a real landlord. A solid and imperturbable individual, he has a bluff though kindly manner, a nose like a ripe strawberry, and his many years of witnessing the worst side of human nature have somehow not soured his outlook on life. Although not given to ostentatious display of wealth, he carries a wad of ready cash which would choke a pelican, and has the respect of both licensees and customers throughout the city. It is said that, despite his advancing years, he has never had to call the police for help in removing troublemakers from his two pubs, and his technique for discreetly giving them something to remember him by as they hurtle through the door is much admired in the trade. He is clearly a good, honest and open man, and has already called me several times to see if he can be of help as I settle in. I think I shall learn much about pubmanship from him, and if the Ship Leopard prospers half as well as his two little goldmines, I shall be more than content.

*   *   *   *   *

Yet another miserable evening session, and I am beginning to wonder if I have made a fatal career move. I am now on my seventeenth profession, and time is getting short for me to find contentment for myself, and some sort of future security for my wife. I left school without bothering to wait for any qualifications, and have still not found my true métier. In spite of a run of setbacks and reversals, I have remained optimistic, and always felt that I was just marking time until my ability was recognised by the rest of the world, so it would not matter too much what I did in the meantime. In hard times I have turned my hand to gravedigging, factory work and delivering beer as well as drinking quite a lot of it. Then there were our attempts at setting up family concerns like the pickled onion manufacturing company and a lonely hearts club. For a while, I was even a dressmaker's assistant, until we were stitched up by a false friend.

Generally, I have enjoyed everything I have done for a living until I have learned to do it, then boredom and discontent have set in and I have had to come up with a new way of keeping my mind occupied and making ends meet while waiting for real success to arrive. And all the time my wife has been foursquare behind me, putting up with the hard times and being full of enthusiasm for every crazy proposal I have made. I have dragged her from one financial crisis to the next, and still she has smiled bravely and supported me in everything that I have tried to do. I do not know of any couples happier to be together than us, but the trick of making money and keeping hold of it seems to have passed me by. I know that love of a good and faithful woman is much more important than having a positive bank balance, but I would dearly like to have both for my wife's sake. She does not need convincing that I am of worth, but as the inside of the Ship Leopard continues to resemble an empty tomb, I find myself increasingly prey to self-doubt, and even self-pity.

Monday 25th

Another entry for the weird customer register this morning when one of my aged regulars arrived in duplicate. For three weeks I have been bemused by an old codger who comes in every day to cast a miasma of gloom over the public bar. On Mondays, he takes up his position by the juke box just so he can complain about the noise level while he is making his pint of mild last a good hour. On Tuesdays he stands at the other end of the bar, staring gloomily into his pint of bitter and telling anyone who tries to talk to him that he is deaf.

Today I discovered that I have not been dealing with a paranoid schizophrenic, but one half of a pair of identical twins. According to the older regulars, they were born in the side street alongside the Leo, live there still, but lead completely separate lives. One occupies the top half of the house, while the other keeps to the downstairs area. According to legend they fell out over the ownership of a toy trumpet around seventy years ago, and have not got on since. The exception is their monthly visit to the Leo, when they get together to argue about the shared household expenses, and perhaps even the trumpet. It is said that there is a story behind every door in the most ordinary street, but I am now convinced that there is something special about this area, and particularly the people who choose to use the Ship Leopard Tavern.

Doing the Rounds

The tradition of drinking 'by the round' dates back to the 18th century, when a peculiar device was introduced to try and curb excessive indulgence. A huge wooden tankard fitted with pegs marking out half-pint measures would be passed around the tavern, with each customer drinking to the next mark down. The expression 'taking someone down a peg or two' thus derives from the common practice of getting one over on the next person in the round by depriving him of his fair share...

FEBRUARY

The bank manager called this morning to observe that we are continuing to attract a remarkable range of international celebrities. Quite apart from the initial visits and markers from Messrs M. Mouse and A. Einstein, it seems Mahatma Ghandi has chosen to use the Leo as a clearing house for his cheques. I promised to talk to the staff again, and tore up the IOU from one Mustapha Pint that Twiggy Bristols accepted in good faith last night.

Before we arrived, I had no idea that running a corner local also included acting as banker, credit controller and financial consultant. I am getting better at refusing credit facilities, but made some bad errors of judgement in the early days. Sadly, one of them was trying to re-institute the tradition of running a slate. The idea was that I would advance customers credit in the form of drinks during the week, then they would settle up on pay day. It is a system which has worked in British locals for centuries, but the past is obviously a different country as far as many of my customers are concerned. The traditional practice of using a blackboard to register debts proved to be unsatisfactory when it was wiped clean in alleged error by a member of the darts team, and everyone I asked denied they had ever been on the list.

A method involving straight loans in exchange for promisory notes was also a washout, as most of the people I did business with at the beginning of the month have never returned. I have even had some of my shadier visitors trying to introduce a barter system, and been offered anything from items of clothing and any number of car radios to a complete three-piece suite in exchange for cash or a drinks tab. The radios usually have wires hanging from the back and screwdriver marks around the edges, so it's obvious they are not the legitimate property of the vendor.

When I asked about the colour and design of the three-piece suite, the character offering it asked me what size and shape I would prefer. If nothing else, I am a quick learner, so have now developed a system of taking pledges in the form of wrist watches. The routine is that the customer hands over his timepiece when he is short of funds, and I advance him credit until he redeems it on pay day. At the start of the week, the shelf behind the bar servery looks like a pawnbroker's shop window, but the arrangement works well as I am now quite an expert at valuation and ensuring I only advance a fraction of the value of each item. Yesterday, a shifty-looking type came in and opened his briefcase with a dramatic flourish on the bar. It was full of obviously phoney designer watches, which he said he could let me have at wholesale price. I merely pointed at my back shelf and asked him if he would like to buy some real ones.

Tuesday 3rd

It is not yet 7am, and I have already been hard at it for an hour, sorting out the empties and re-stocking the shelves with bottles. We have a cleaning lady, but I must see about getting a potman to come in for the early shift. I must also ask my wife about a number of empty pet food tins I found in the dustbin in the yard. I have promised her a pub cat, but have not had the time to arrange it yet. Hopefully, she has been feeding a stray, but knowing how she feels about our move and some of our customers, I am glad I have not tried any of the darts team's sandwiches.

Wednesday 4th

According to my calculations, we almost made a profit today. Or at least, almost broke even. Apart, that is, from the shortfall in the cash register. The headcount at peak trading was well into double figures (though not, admittedly, at the same time), and we must have served more than fifty customers in total. Some of those were also return visits.

With so many outlets in the area, the local drinkers tend to graze from pub to pub, and I must think of some way of keeping them here so that we can build an atmosphere. It is a particularly curious pub paradox that most customers prefer to drink where it is busy rather than where they can take their pick of the seating and be served in a trice. This rule does not, of course, apply to my collection of aged regulars, who relish having the place to themselves and enjoy my courtship of their meagre contributions to the economy. Now that January is behind us, I feel I can concentrate on building the business, though it will take some time yet for us to feel settled after the big disruption to our lives.

Anyone who has moved home will know what a traumatic experience a change of address can be. To get the feel of taking over at a pub, imagine moving in to a house at exactly the same time as the previous owner leaves, then having to start a new business in your front room the same morning.

On our big day, we sat in the public bar watching domestic items of furniture pass on the stairs and wondering what the future hours and years would hold as we waited for the rival brokers to arrive for the official handing-over process. From the start, it seemed to me that they were far too friendly, and as we shook hands, both looked at me with what appeared to be a mixture of sympathy and faint contempt.

Every single item of stock in hand now had to be listed and the individual amounts and measures agreed upon, with me paying the wholesale price to complete the deal. After casually assessing the contents of part-full spirit bottles by eye and kicking the odd barrel in the cellar in a decidedly cavalier manner, my man came out of a huddle with the outgoing landlord's agent and announced that a satisfactory deal had been arranged. I signed yet another huge cheque, and they disappeared without a backward glance. As if to add insult to injury, they could be heard laughing over some private joke in the passageway, and discussing where they could find a good pub to have lunch together.

Suddenly it was opening time, and my first ever session behind the bar of the Ship Leopard Tavern went by in a blur. I did not have time to feel nervous as the place seemed as busy as during the Christmas period. Sitting in the bar with my wife afterwards, I said this was a good omen and showed the customers were keen to support their new host. She was not so enthusiastic, and said the huge crowd might have more to do with the advertisement in the local paper that all the drinks were free for the first two hours. Going by the cheques and pledges in the cash register, some of our customers were obviously delighted to have also found a new banker, and one who did not make a service or interest charge. Holding a piece of paper up for my inspection, my wife also commented dryly that she doubted we would see Mr. M. Mouse again.

Friday 6th

I appear to be suffering from what Tez the Prez calls the Last Landlord Syndrome. At least once a session, a regular will say how wonderful the place was under the control of the previous landlord, and by implication compare me unfavourably with my predecessor. Not only did the beer taste better, but the place was always packed with deliriously happy and free-spending customers, there was always the warmest of welcomes, and the weather outside was considerably better. I know this cannot be true, but it is another depressing example of the darker side of human nature. Some of my customers seem determined to make me pay for taking their money.

Monday 9th

An unpleasant end to the evening with a scuffle in the public bar. Luckily the two combatants were both well over 60, so it came to nothing. The trouble started during a pool league fixture when our captain leaned over to make the vital stroke and win the match. As he lined up for his shot, his false teeth fell out and struck the object ball, and the opposition called a foul. After I had restored order, there was a long debate and it was finally agreed that the shot could be replayed, this time with our man's teeth safely in his back pocket.

Tuesday 10th

Another miserable morning, with the twin Brothers Grim and other assorted walking dead making the lounge bar look like God's waiting room. I chose the Ship Leopard because I wanted to prove that the death of the corner local is not inevitable, but at least half my regulars won't need next year's calendar, and I can see why this sort of pub is in terminal decline. To be honest, I have not frequented a local like the Leo for many years, and realise now that not all pub customers spend as freely as me, or want the same sort of services and surroundings. I have always prided myself on being working class, and believed the regulars would respond to me giving them a cosy home-from-home. Either their homes are not like mine, or they just don't want what I am trying to offer. Perhaps they actually prefer a pub where nobody speaks to them and they are left alone to look morosely into their glasses and think how badly life has treated them. Perhaps I should have followed my wife's suggestion, and looked harder for a country pub with potential.

At the start of the project, we visited and enquired about a number of pretty little rural outlets, but the takings were always abysmal and I felt it would be an uphill struggle being located in the middle of nowhere and stuck with the same customers day after day. Now I am stuck with the same customers every day in a seedy inner city location, and the strangers who visit us often bring the whiff of trouble with them.

Apart from my desire to recreate the classic corner local, fear of failure was the reason I chose to set up business in a busy area. After seeing how many customers regularly use the strip and calculating what they must be spending, it seemed to me that I could do a much better job than the other landlords in the area at capturing the available trade. I trust I have not made the classic civilian's error of thinking that any rundown pub in a heavily populated area is a potential goldmine. I hope I am just feeling low, but with each day it seems more and more certain that the Leo and my plans for reviving its fortunes are cursed.

Monday 16th

We held our first proper staff meeting today. My original idea was that we would meet regularly after work to get to know each other in a relaxed atmosphere and explore ways of doing better business. Unfortunately, my helpers just seem to want to disappear as soon as their shifts are over, or have had too much to drink to make any sensible suggestions.

They are, to say the least, a mixed bunch. Before I took over, I was told by the outgoing landlord that the law required me to keep the existing members of staff on the payroll. Despite what he had previously said about the need to watch them and the till, he then claimed they were all loyal, reliable and an asset to the business. He could have taken them with him to his new business, he said, but thought it best to let me keep them as they knew the ropes and would be able to help me settle in. After six weeks of working with them, I think he was having a joke on me, and was glad to leave them behind.

The youngest and most promising member of the team is Twiggy Bristols, who is for obvious reasons also the most popular with any customers who still have an interest in the opposite sex. There is also a lady of indeterminate age called Dolly who seems to be almost completely deaf, and a totally neurotic divorcee called Anne. Despite her affliction, Dolly refuses to wear her hearing aid, which has led to some interesting confusion when drinks are ordered. To some people it would be amusing, but I have to pay for the mistakes when a customer orders a packet of pork scratchings and gets a port and lemon.

Desperate Anne (as the wags in the public bar know her) seems to be continually ill or stressed-out, and calls in sick more often than putting in her invariably dramatic and tearful performance. When she is on duty, she spends her time either ignoring the customers while staring soulfully into space, or disappearing to the Ladies when anybody upsets her. Ironically, Anne claims she took the job at the Leo to get out of the house, mix with people and face up to making a new life for herself after the sudden departure of her husband with their milkman. This morning, a customer asked quite politely for a pint of lager and blackcurrant and she immediately disappeared in a flood of tears. When I remarked to Twiggy I had not realised how sensitive Anne was about the gruesome mixtures some of our customers order, she explained that Dracula's Blood was the favourite tipple of Anne's former husband, and she cannot bear to be reminded of their happy times together before the milkman came between them. The only consolation is that Desperate Anne seems to put all her wages into the jukebox so she can listen to a suitably wailing lament and feel even more unhappy, so I suppose it could be argued I am getting her services for free. Hearing *I Will Always Love You* more than fourteen times a session, however, seems a high price to pay for the savings.

Making up my permanent staff list is a middle-aged, seedy and morose bachelor known to the regulars as Dirty Barry. He insists on calling himself my bars manager, though the only thing he appears to manage well is upsetting the customers and the rest of the staff. He also seems to think an important part of his job is the screening of potential customers, and will only serve them if he approves of their application for a drink. Along with his unappetising personality, he has a very bad case of foot and body odour. Like a lot of small people, he can be overbearing and even aggressive, and we have had some near misses with potentially dangerous confrontations. Dirty Barry appears to know no fear when taking on a troublesome person or crowd, and luckily, his victims generally seem so astonished at his level of aggression that they do not retaliate. On our first Friday night, a large and obnoxious stag party rampaged through the doors of the public bar, and they were obviously bent on enjoying themselves to the full by making everyone else unhappy. I found urgent business in the cellar as the noise grew to a crescendo, then the banging of the outer pub door and shouting in the street told me it was safe to return. When I asked Barry how he managed to get rid of them without blood being spilled, he calmly explained he had told them I was a twenty stone kung-fu expert and an ex-heavyweight amateur boxing champion into the bargain, and that if they didn't leave quietly he was going to call on me to sort them out.

I tried to suggest a less confrontational approach for the future, but he seemed more concerned that they had had the audacity to take their glasses with them as they piled out of the pub and on to the street. Were we not, he asked, going to pursue them and reclaim our property? I carefully explained that I did not think that would be a good idea, and issued some new instructions. From now on, all stag night parties would be charged a standard twenty pence for every ice cube put in their glasses. The drink-befuddled mobs would never know about the surcharge, and it would give us some small degree of revenge. A cowardly way out, perhaps, but better to lose a glass than get it in the face.

I had heard about the stag night problem on the strip before taking over at the Leo, but had not dreamed it would be this bad, and now dread Friday and Saturday nights. The packs of young men who regularly come crashing through the doors are allegedly seeing a friend off into married life in the traditional manner, but I think most of them are just looking for an excuse to wreak havoc for a few hours. What makes it worse is our location. We are number nine on the run, and the revellers leave their brains and all traces of social responsibility at number seven. Their final port of call is the Black Dog, which is a notorious pub at the end of the strip. From what I have heard of the place, the normal behaviour level is such that anything short of a full-pitched battle goes unnoticed. Tez warned me about the weekly stag runs when we first met, and said that all the landlords in the area call Friday and Saturday evenings Planet of the Apes nights. Apart from recommending the surcharge on the ice cubes, he also advised me to get some revenge by adding what he called a headache toll. Traditionally, each stag party will have a getting-legless fund, and elect one of their more reliable members to hold the money pot and buy all the drinks. When serving him with a huge round, the trick is to tally up the bill, then add on at least twenty percent of the total. Provided you show no hesitation and make the sum convincingly precise rather than a suspiciously round number, the amount is never queried. It is small compensation for being terrorised every weekend, but at least it is some measure of revenge. After our first Friday night I considered employing door stewards for the weekend, but Tez the Prez says that they are not only expensive, but can also start more trouble than they prevent. Bouncers on the door are an irresistible challenge to any group of marauding thugs with money in their pockets and a belly full of beer. Perhaps I should appoint Deaf Dolly as the only person to serve stag groups in the hope that they will become so frustrated with trying to get the right drinks that they will move on to their next port of call.

Given the choice, Twiggy is the only member of staff whose services I would have retained. She is obviously an asset as the younger regulars seem to come in just to be served by her. The drawback is that she tends to ignore the older or uglier customers, and seems to spend a lot of her time hanging over the bar and entertaining her latest boyfriend. Today it was a Ricky. He looks exactly like all the others in her retinue, says he is some sort of salesman, and is very flash. The first thing he does on arrival is toss his shiny and very obvious BMW key ring casually on the bar, tell everyone how much money he has made that day, and complain about the traffic on the motorway from London. What he doesn't know is that I looked outside when he came in early this evening, and the only vehicles in our part of the street were an old Ford Fiesta and a bicycle chained to my drainpipe. At a suitable moment when Twiggy is listening raptly to his boasting, I shall ask him which one is his.

Wednesday 18th

The street outside is lined with parked cars, but the owners must have been visiting other pubs along the strip. I have noticed that the few customers who come by car to the Leopard seem to have a very relaxed attitude to drinking and driving, and act as if the breathalyser has not yet been invented. I read yesterday that the relatives of a man killed in a crash in America sued the owner of the bar where he did most of his drinking, and won huge damages. If that ever becomes the situation here, I am sure it will put many pubs in Britain out of business. More and more people nowadays are getting away with blaming somebody else for their misfortunes, while it seems to me that we should all take responsibility for our actions. I do, however, try to see that nobody drinks more than is good for them whilst on my premises. This evening, I refused to serve a customer who could hardly stand, and after he staggered out of the door, I asked his drinking companion if he were not going to see his friend safely home. The man shrugged and said it would be okay as his mate didn't live far away, and anyway had his car with him.

Friday 20th

A better evening, though it cost me a few pounds to learn the rules of a fascinating pub game. A trio of car dealers call in on their way to the fleshpots of the seafront strip on Fridays, and tonight they taught me how to play Spoof. As a keen student of human nature, I found it fascinating. The basic rules consist of players selecting and hiding any number of coins in their fists, then taking it in turns to guess what the group total is. After they have made their calls, the players open their hands and a tally is made to see if anyone has got it right. Last night, I managed to make the correct bid on three occasions, while the other players were wildly out in their estimations. This meant I had to buy all the drinks, but I enjoyed studying their faces and working out what number of coins they would opt for. Afterwards, it occurred to me how unlike the game is from any other which is played for stakes, as success is actually penalised. I suggested to one of the dealers that it would be better if the caller making the right guess were to drop out, leaving the others to battle on and the least successful player to buy the round. He said he had heard of the game being played that way, but this variation was a particular house rule at the Leo, and a tradition. I agreed with him that traditions should be maintained, but in future I think the Ship Leopard will adopt the internationally agreed regulations.

Monday 23rd

An unpleasant incident this lunchtime when Old Joe notched up another victim for Nosher, his ferocious Jack Russell terrier. On the day we arrived, I took exception to a filthy old armchair taking up drinking room at the bar, and told Dirty Barry to get rid of it. He explained that it belonged to an aged regular, and that nobody was allowed to sit in or move it. He added that the owner came in twice every day and saw off three pints of Pompey Royal and two double rums during each visit. After some rapid calculations about the weekly net worth of the chair to my turnover, I made my first executive decision at the Leo and said that Joe's special chair could stay exactly where it was.

Like every local I have ever used, the Leo has a collection of aged regulars, but they all seem easy to handle compared with Joe. A short, thickset man with one leg, a shock of white hair, puce complexion and an impressive range of scowls, he arrives by taxi at the same time every day, and immediately sets about taking over his territory. Having disposed of any customers in his personal exclusion zone with no more than a glare, he will put the money for his first pint on the bartop and stare unflinchingly at the pump as it is pulled. The process is repeated at ten minute intervals during his stay, and since we met he has resisted all my attempts to engage him in conversation. The only time he speaks to anyone is when a stranger gets too close, and is unmoved by the ensuing scowls, grunts and offensive body language.

This is always the cue for Joe to heave himself up, announce his intention of going to the toilet and ask the stranger to hold the dog's lead. If the customer is an animal lover and rash enough to try and pat or smooth it, the dog will bite him. Before my arrival at the Leopard, this was Nosher's regular party trick, and the only time I have seen Old Joe smile was when he returned to find blood had been drawn. The first time it happened, I thought it was an accident, and it cost me a taxi to hospital as well as a customer. After today's victim had been claimed, I had a quiet word with Joe and he grudgingly agreed to discontinue the practice. He is obviously an old rascal, but I think we understand each other, and his consumption rate means he makes a valuable contribution to our struggle to make ends meet.

My admiration for his capacity increased even more today when his taxi driver told me that, after visiting us, he goes on to the local British Legion club for some really serious drinking.

What's Yours?

The most popular pub drink in Victorian times was mild ale, which by then had replaced a weak form of stout known as porter. Mild was sold at four pence for a quart (2 pints) measure, so the seedier taverns became known as 'four ale bars' though they often only sold one. The average yearly consumption of alcohol in those times was reckoned to be about 30 gallons of beer and one gallon of spirits. Allowing for infants, the infirm and the rare non-drinker, this means that the serious pub-goer was working his or her way through the alcoholic equivalent of fifteen pints of beer every day.

The strongest beer ever (officially) brewed was created in 1985 at The Frog and Parrot in Sheffield. With an alcoholic content of 16.9 percent (average beer is around the 3 percent mark) it was most suitably named 'Roger and Out'...

MARCH

Sunday morning finds me in the cellar, anxiously checking the sell-by dates on my barrels.

As I climb through the trap and back into the bar, I can hear the toll of a distant bell and reflect upon the long and uncomfortable relationship between pub and church. Wherever you go in the English countryside, you will find a pub nestling almost in the shadow of the village church, and the two establishments were for many centuries the focal point of the community. Some were connected with underground passages, and social historians still argue whether they were originally dug for the use of the congregation, or for the landlord to discreetly provide the parson with refreshment after he had shouted himself dry condemning the evil of strong drink during the Sunday sermon. Nowadays, the relationship between church and pub is less strained, and both establishments are trying to attract an ever-diminishing audience.

*   *   *   *   *

We had more fun and games with stag parties last night. Not only do they arrive and depart like a Viking raiding party in a particularly bad mood, what they drink is enough to put my decent customers off their beer. Last week it was Dracula's Blood and now it seems a mixture of cider and bitter is the favourite way of inducing a satisfactory berserker state. After the departure of the final group, Dirty Barry told me we had a problem with the toilet door. When I asked if it had been damaged, he explained that the problem was that it had disappeared. We found it on top of a car a little further along the strip this morning, but have not so

41

far solved the mystery of how it was smuggled out through the public bar.

Monday 2nd

A strange encounter with a new customer whom I first took to be a Serbo-Croat fresh off the back of a lorry coming out of the local ferryport. It was only with Dirty Barry's translatory services that I discovered our visitor lives round the corner and was actually speaking his own very personal version of English.

I was born near the city and have lived here all my life, but even I have a problem understanding the most extreme examples of local dialect. A friend who lectures in linguistics at the university believes that the weird accent and argot favoured by locals is a result of generations of people from other parts of the country and Empire arriving to join the navy and settling here. The resulting pattern of pronunciation and accent is a strange hybrid, with variations in different parts of the city, and sometimes in different streets. Overall, it comes out as a sort of westcountry twang with south London overtones, and to a stranger, it must sound like someone doing a bad impression of Long John Silver and Reggie Kray at the same time. It is also a local tradition that every sentence ends with a question mark, and a mixture of naval slang, Romany and cockney rhyming patois is often thrown in for good measure and to confuse outsiders. Our new regular also has a speech impediment, and what will happen when he asks Deaf Dolly for a Brown Split I dread to think. One consolation is that the foul language which punctuates his every sentence will be unrecognisable to my more refined customers and hardly likely to cause offence to the majority. If I installed a swearbox and could make the worst offenders in the public bar use it, I think I would be able to retire in a year.

Wednesday 4th

Athough it seems hardly credible, business is even worse.

I had hoped that trade would get better when the dead months following Christmas had struggled by and the winter broken, but now my staff outnumber customers at most times, and the off-licence door opens only to admit a chill wind or a tradesman anxious for me to settle his account. The fairy lights above the bar glow glumly through the ranks of unused glasses on the back counter, and there has not even been a fight to liven the place up.

For me, the boredom is almost as bad as the silence of the tills. Yet another pub truism I have learned since arriving at the Leo is that the quieter trade is, the more the landlord needs to be at home to entertain and hopefully delay the few punters who venture in. But there are, or should be, limits. Infuriatingly, all my regulars seem to think I have nothing better to do than hang around the bar in case they choose to drop in. What makes it worse is my wife reminding me how irritated I used to be at arriving in a local and finding the landlord absent without my leave. She also claims I have made a rod for my own back by treating the lounge bar like the stage of the London Palladium during our rare busy sessions, but I think she exaggerates. It is true I like to put on a show for my customers, but it is hard going now that there are so few of them. They drop in when they like, and expect me to be on my best form when it suits them. Then, more often than not, they want to talk at rather than with me. It is very hard to keep up a façade of interest when someone is telling you about the battery life of his hearing aid. I suspect even a performer of Tom Jones' energy would be hard pushed to keep the adrenalin surging in these circumstances, and certainly not for hours on end.

In truth, I am finding it increasingly difficult to appear interested in my regular customers' trivial concerns, and especially their attitude that I and the pub are only here for their convenience and entertainment. Lately, I have been allowing my mask of banal amiability to slip, and it has led to some unpleasant situations. I have also concluded that it is not always surly and unsociable people who choose to be landlords. They probably become so because of having to deal with the Great British Public. At least, that is true in my case. Now that I am being paid to be a host and cannot pick and choose my guests, I find it increasingly difficult to sparkle every moment I am on duty. Last week was a typical example, when a middle-aged couple who arrive most days to swell my profits with the proceeds from two halves of lager shandy and a packet of crisps (they ask for a complete rundown of every flavour yet *always* choose Spring Onion) came in. After negotiating their order, they had the cheek to complain that I had not been there to greet them during their state visit of the day before. I was completely sober at that time of day, but rather than making a simpering apology as I would have done just a month ago, I lost my temper, and fetched a hammer and some six-inch nails from the shed in the yard. Handing them to the husband, I invited him to secure my feet firmly to the floor so he could be sure I would be in place and ready for their next visit. There followed an awkward silence as a shadow passed across his face and the other regulars started taking an interest. Then I saw a way out for both of us and smiled and gave what my wife calls my totally false laugh. He and his wife joined in, and I discovered a way of releasing my frustrations without losing my trade or my teeth. Since that encounter, I have been developing my skills at insulting customers by telling them the truth and getting away with it by pretending to be joking. It is a fine art, and I am only practicing it on those I think will accept it. However, I shall not try the technique on our huge and very boring barrow boy regular Monster Ted till I am more confident of the outcome.

Thursday 5th

My first night away from the Ship Leopard in nearly nine weeks. Tez the Prez tells me that publicans usually have either Tuesday or Wednesday nights off duty as this is the quietest time of the week. Paradoxically, most of them spend the precious hours away from their own bars doing the rounds of other people's pubs. I have even heard it is not uncommon for some landlords to spend more time on other licensed premises than on their own, which seems a funny way of doing business. Apart from needing a night away from the Leo and the few regulars likely to be on duty, I thought it would be a good idea to see just how well or hopefully badly my competitors are doing. My companion was Dirty Barry the bars manager, who has now appointed himself as my minder. He is a good foot shorter than me, but very loyal and has taken to following me like a faithful terrier everywhere I go inside the pub. I felt uneasy about leaving the Leo without a man behind the bar, but my wife agreed to keep an eye on things and I left an itinerary so she could call me if there were any problems or in the unlikley event of Dolly and Twiggy Bristols becoming too busy to cope. To combine business with pleasure, I decided to follow the traditional stag night route, starting with a pub no more than half a mile from the Leo, yet with seven others in between.

Along what the regulars call the strip are a variety of inns, taverns, bars and 'fun' pubs for youngsters, where the only fun seems to lie in guessing how much the place can get away with charging for the drinks, and forecasting when the next fight will break out. It was a novel experience visiting other licensed premises and seeing what was going on there from my new perspective as a professional landlord. Most of the licensees and managers were on duty, and seemed only too happy to tell me their troubles. They also seemed happy to tell me that they admired my courage in taking on the Leo, from where they said the previous licensee had been trying to escape for years. When I brought up the subject of the stag night problem, however, I found little agreement or sympathy from the licensees at the start of the route. One self-satisfied landlord whose premises are number three on the run said that the groups are reasonably well-behaved when they reach him, spend a lot of money in a short time, then move on to cause problems at someone else's pub. I thought about pointing out that I was the someone else whose pub was being regularly put under siege by customers inflamed by the drink he had sold them, but there was no point in starting a row. Overall, we had a convivial night, and I learned a little more about Dirty Barry during our pub run. He is a strange and sometimes intense man, with no friends or apparent interest in the opposite sex, which is just as well considering his personal hygiene problems. He told me he lives alone in a bed sitter and is a country and western music fan. He is also a rabid supporter of the local football team, which taken together with his job at the Leo shows he is obviously a supporter of lost causes. I asked him about girlfriends, and he said he tried sex once in 1979 and didn't like it, so has not bothered since.

We ended our evening at the Black Dog, and to my chagrin it was busier than the Ship Leopard at Christmas. The noise and behaviour level was also such that the vilest of my stag night visitors would go unnoticed. I recognised a few of my more disreputable public bar customers, and some that I had actually barred. Most of the female customers looked too young to be out on their own at that time of night, and the older ones looked as if they should have been on duty under the nearest street lamp. Presiding over his unsavoury if highly successful domain was the infamous landlord, Casser Blygh. Although we have not met, I have heard many tales of his shady activities from my customers, and if half of them are true, he should be licensee of the Jamaica Inn rather than the Black Dog. A gross giant of a man, he looks like he was poured from the mould before the mixture was properly set. In contrast to his lumpen and shapeless body, the licensee of the Dog has somehow disturbingly small and neat features, with a button nose, invisible ears and a tiny rosebud mouth. His calculating eyes are barely visible through the swollen flesh of his heavily veined face, but they followed me like a cat watching a grounded sparrow as we fought our way to the bar. He did not bother to shift from his position on a stool at the end of the bar, but gave me a patronising nod to show he knew who I was. He then leaned across the counter and said something to his ring of cronies that made them laugh. Rarely have I met someone who I have disliked so much on sight. He is the unchallenged king of the strip, and obviously regards me as no threat to his position, but I shall do my best to unseat him.

Just before closing time, the landlord heaved himself from the stool to perform his nightly party trick and remind his customers and rival publicans how successful he is compared with them. Waddling behind the bar, he lifted the flap of the cash register and peered inside. With a smug smile and a glance at me, he then took a piece of chalk and wrote the day's takings on a blackboard hanging below the clock. If the amount claimed was true, he is taking more in a day than we are in a week. I have already learned that all landlords lie about their cash turnover, but Casser Blygh undoubtedly runs one of the busiest pubs in the city. The bell rang, and to avoid giving our host the additional pleasure of asking for our glasses, I told Barry to drink up, and we slunk down the wind-swept strip to discover if the headcount at the Ship Leopard had reached double figures for the night. I would love to have a tenth of the number of regular customers who flock to pay court to the landlord of the Dog, but given the sort of people who patronise the place, I would still rather have my pub than his.

*　　*　　*　　*　　*

I have arrived back from my evening off to discover we have a pub dog. After examining the till and finding that I had spent more on the night out than we had taken over the counter, I checked that all the exits were locked and the toilet door still in place, then made my way upstairs. Having reached the landing and switched on the light, I found myself confronting a hound only slightly smaller than a Shetland pony. The creature looked like a cross between a wolf and a great dane and appeared to be a dirty grey colour, with very white and obviously strong teeth.

After considering the situation for a moment, I retired down the stairs to collect some packets of crisps, then returned to attempt to win its favour. As I made my nervous offering, the beast remained motionless, regarding me with the steady gaze I have seen on nature programmes as a lion considers whether to ignore a potential victim or make the effort to tear it to shreds. It is also the same look I have received from the more dangerous sub-humans I have ejected from the public bar. After the crisps were ignored and the situation seemed to have reached an impasse, I gave up trying to befriend the creature, and had to call for my wife's assistance. She eventually appeared, summed up the situation and snapped her fingers, and the huge creature lolloped to her side to fawn over her.

When she had calmed me down with a large brandy, my wife explained that her new pet had arrived in the bar that evening with its owner, a Royal Marine who had been posted unexpectedly abroad. The man had said that, though it would break his heart, there was nobody who he could trust to look after his beloved dog properly, so he would be going on a final visit to the vet in the morning. My wife could not bear to see this happen, and Tyson is now a permanent non-paying guest at the Leo. She has promised me he will be no trouble and insists that, despite his appearance, he has never actually killed a human being. After a brief debate which I knew I could not win, I had to agree that I had promised my wife a dog and cat to keep her company while I am occupied with building trade at the Leo.

To be fair and remembering my reaction to his appearance, he will also be a most effective deterrent to any would-be burglars or troublemakers. Perhaps I will try him out on a stag night party this weekend, and see if he finds any of the guests to his taste.

Monday 9th

Our pub dog is not only a coward, but a hopeless alcoholic. I discovered these character defects after his first appearance in the bar while Old Joe and his tiny terrier were in residence. My wife had opened the door to tell me she was taking Tyson for his daily walk to the butcher's shop, and brought him in to make friends with Nosher. The confrontation lasted no more than seconds, and resulted in my alleged devil dog taking refuge in the cellar. Like much of the pond life and potential troublemakers I have to deal with on a daily basis, Tyson looks ferocious but has no stomach for a fight when challenged. I have also discovered that he spends most of his day in an alcoholic haze. This morning I caught him drinking the slops out of a bucket in the yard, and a regular has told me the true state of affairs. Tyson's former owner is well-known in the pub community, and he has never been a Royal Marine. Far from having a last drink with his beloved dog before going to serve his country, he was anticipating serving a stiff sentence for passing forged notes in the local pubs, a charge on which he was out on bail. Tyson is famous throughout the area for his addiction to alcohol and spinelessness, and apart from having a useless guard dog, I am apparently the laughing stock of the strip.

To add to my humiliation, my informant told me that it is common knowledge that my wife gave the con man £200 for what he said was a valuable and highly trained guard dog.

I just hope she paid him from the till with some of the dud notes he had passed over the bar during my absence.

Friday 13th

Our accountant has been for his monthly visit, and the news is not good. Originally, we were supposed to meet no more than three or four times a year, but having seen my attempts at book-keeping, he now thinks it best we get together more frequently so he can help us with the clerical side of the business. On paper, the financial ins and outs of running a pub are very straightforward, but in practice they are more complex. With what is known as the 'wet trade' part of our takings, we buy the drinks we need at less than half the price at which we sell them. By 'marking up' the wholesale price to the right level, one is supposed to arrive at a satisfactory margin after allowing for wastage and other losses through bad practices or pilfering by staff. If we had any food or 'dry' trade apart from the odd packet of crisps or meat pie, the proceeds from those sales would be added to the pot. The difference between what we pay for our goods and what we sell them for is known as the gross profit. To deduct from this figure there are of course the costs, which include the monthly rental to the brewery, heating, light, insurance, rates, maintenance and the staff wages. What is left after deducting our overheads from our gross profit figure is, as our accountant said with some degree of irony, all ours after income tax and repayments on loans or other expenses. Even though we are not as yet drawing any wages, we are, our financial mentor says, currently subsidising the running of the pub by several hundred pounds a week.

This was not the idea, and it seems very unfair as we are both working very hard and for long hours. When we sat in pubs around the city and saw what they were charging and worked out the profit ratio, it seemed that many licensees were making a small fortune. According to our accountant, though, we are actually paying to work our hundred hours a week at the Ship Leopard.

After delivering the bad news he added insult to injury by giving us a lecture about exercising tighter control over costs. As if pulling a rabbit out of a hat, he then told us what we already know; our problem is not so much about outgoings as ingoings. In essence, we need to attract more customers and sell more drinks. Without, of course, increasing our costs. I noticed that his suggestions for cutting back on overheads did not include dispensing with his services, and that he made sure I settled his latest invoice before he left.

As he disappeared with our cheque, I also noticed he was walking quickly, as if hurrying on his way to the bank to clear it before it was too late.

Monday 16th

More bad financial news when I emptied the fruit machine in the public bar this morning. The prize hopper was empty, and the cash box contains a large number of leaden discs and a handful of foreign coins, including a dozen French ten franc pieces. I took little comfort from knowing that the rate of exchange is such that the francs are actually worth more than the pound coin they replace, so the cheaters have cheated themselves for a change.

If there is a new way to fiddle the fruit machine, my public bar customers are sure to discover it. Last month it was a coin on a wire to steal unlimited free plays, and now we have the lead poisoning. The situation is especially worrying, as the fruit machine is supposed to provide a vital part of our income and I know that in some busy pubs, machine income can pay the rent. We have our own small clique of fruit machine enthusiasts who are obviously addicted to playing them, and watching their antics provides me with another fascinating example of human behaviour. Apart from those hopeless slaves who don't care if anyone is watching them waste their money, most serious players don't want to display their weakness and will get up to all sorts of antics to pretend they are not hooked. Like round-dodgers, some affect the need to go to the toilet frequently, casually slipping a coin in the machine as they pass. They do the same on the way back and some will make the journey a dozen times a session. Having invested so heavily, they then congregate at the part of the bar nearest the machine and dare it to pay out to someone else. If another regular player wins the measly jackpot, they have to pretend to be happy for his or her good fortune. If a stranger happens to win, they join together in mutual outrage, especially if the winner doesn't immediately feed all the coins straight back into the machine.

Curiously, our most valuable machine player is a retired accountant who of all people should know just how bad the odds are on winning anything. His fruitless battle with the fruit machine is worth about £50 a week to me, and I was not pleased to learn this morning that Dirty Barry has barred him for constantly using up all the small change in the till.

Thursday 19th

It is Giro day, so at least the public bar will be busy this lunchtime. I sometimes wonder why I and my wife are bothering to work so hard, as some of my unemployed regulars seem better off than we are at the end of the week. Before I became a licensee, I had a degree of sympathy for those who have to suffer the indignity

51

of letting the rest of us support them. Now I see that many are quite happy to make a career out of not working. Like lifers in prison they seem to have become institutionalised, and those who use my pub fall into two main categories. The first kind are the basically unemployable, who are content to live a quiet life and draw their money at the post office over the road before coming in to celebrate the receipt of another dole cheque. The senior members of this club have been on what they call the Old King Cole for years, and are waiting patiently till their income from the state becomes an official pension. They just want to be left alone, and often come in to drown their sorrows and complain bitterly when they receive a letter saying that a job may have been found for them.

The second category includes those with higher aspirations and more expensive lifestyles, who see the unemployment benefit as supplement to their other money-earning activities. At the Leo, we have window cleaners, car dealers and even professional money-lenders who are also drawing unemployment benefit. One regularly plays the stock market with his spare cash and has given me some useful tips. These entrepreneurial types live in constant fear that an offer of official employment will crop up and threaten their full-time career paths. Even allowing for the amount of time I stand around behind the bar with nothing to do, I don't think I would get away with signing on for the jobless benefit.

Perhaps I shall lobby for a subsidy for publicans. If farmers can get it when what they provide is surplus to requirements, why not unsuccessful landlords?

Monday 23rd

I am due a visit from the brewery's area manager, or as he says he is now to be addressed, my Personal Business Development Manager.

In my grandfather's time the brewery agent arrived on his bike every now and then to check that the pub was still there and that the licensee was selling his company's beer in reasonable condition.

As long as the rent was paid on time, whatever else happened on the premises was more or less the licensee's business.

Nowadays, the BDM comes in a shiny new car, equipped with a lap top computer and all sorts of electronic gizmos to analyse the takings and percentages and advise on how they can be improved. Cynical licensees say the real purpose of these visits is to try to help the landlord make more money so the brewery can take it away again in the form of increased rent. This may be true, but to be fair, the brewing industry has undergone dramatic changes in recent times, and the modern pub-owning companies and breweries can hardly be expected to take the traditionally casual attitude to their licensees. In the good old days, there were hundreds of small, family-run breweries owning anything from a handful to several hundred public houses which served as guaranteed outlets for their beer. The most profitable ones would be managed directly by the brewery, and the others let off to tenant landlords for a nominal rent. The brewery would make its real money from the huge volume of beer the average pub would get through in the days when many people would rather drink than eat. As long as the publican kept pumping out the beer, the brewery would be content. In those less demanding times, running a local pub was not always seen as a specialist or even a full-time job, and former footballers, policemen and ex-service people like my grandfather would take a corner local as a semi-retirement plan. Few were proper businessmen, and they were generally glad to have the comforting arm of the brewery around their shoulders. Those who worked all hours and made a go of their pubs were often real characters.

With the march of progress the regional breweries were gradually swallowed up by the big operators, and today there are only a relative handful of small independent brewery companies left. Rather than a tenant, I am a leaseholder with a major brewery company, and under the terms of my contract I must buy the bulk of my stock from them and take responsibility for keeping the pub in good condition. If successful, I will be able to sell the lease on to a new licensee and charge him a 'goodwill' fee based on the success and profits of the Ship Leopard during my reign. With some profitable pubs, the lease may change hands for hundreds of thousands of pounds.

The way things are going at the Leo, I could end up having to pay someone to take over.

*　　*　　*　　*　　*

Our Business Development Manager has been and gone, and he looked nearly as worried as the accountant. Before his visit, I think he may have believed that our weekly drinks orders are so low because we have been breaking our contract and buying our beer from elsewhere. Now he has spent a couple of hours in the pub, he has seen just how bad business is. He is a nice enough young man, but has never been on the working side of the bar and drinks only bottled water. Originally, he was full of enthusiasm when I laid out my business plan for upmarketing the Ship Leopard by encouraging a better class of customer. Now he believes that I may be wrong in trying to impose my ideas on the pub, and has advised me to put my plans for turning the public bar into a restaurant on hold. He also thinks I am being too 'fussy' about the sort of customers I can attract. As he said before leaving, any trade is better than none at all, but then he has not been on duty at the Ship Leopard on a Friday night.

The Barons of Brewing

Until the end of the 17th century, most beer was brewed on the premises at ale houses. Seeing the potential for mass marketing, some of the first specialist brewery companies set up business in London, producing the favourite thirst-quencher of market workers, from where 'porter' beer got its name. Following the Beer Act of 1830 which saw the mushrooming of small pubs, the bigger breweries set about building enormous 'gin palaces', where working people could escape from the squalor of their everyday surroundings. This was the beginning of the rise and rise of the so-called beer barons, who swallowed up most of the smaller regionals on their way to controlling vast beer and pub empires.

APRIL

A quarter of the way through my trial year behind bars, and it is time for strong action if we are to survive until Christmas.

Despite the misgivings of our man from the brewery, I am going to get rid of the pool table as the first step in cleaning up the public bar. It is make or break time, and I am never going to attract the class of customers I want if they are frightened off by some of the creatures currently to be found lurking in my public bar. It was always part of my plan to upgrade the seedier areas of the Ship Leopard and introduce proper catering to provide another income source, and I might as well take the plunge before our credit at the bank runs out. My mind was finally made up last week, when I read an article in a trade newspaper about pub violence. It said a survey had concluded that any combination of a pool table, red wallpaper and harsh lighting was almost guaranteed to incite trouble. At the Ship Leopard, the pool table dominates the public bar, and the main lighting source is a neon strip which makes even the least offensive of customers look like an extra in a horror film. The greasy wallpaper is of the Indian restaurant embossed variety, and is a deep shade of red.

Given the normal standard of behaviour before my arrival, the colour was probably chosen so that bloodstains would be less noticeable.

Yesterday, a nasty brawl proved the survey's conclusions were correct, as the pool table was the catalyst, or at least the excuse. The trouble came when a couple of friends fell out over whose turn it was to start a game, and chose to start a fight instead. They didn't do much damage to each other, but ripped the table cloth, broke both my pool cues, and one of them threw a ball through a particularly nice etched glass window in the partition between the public and lounge bars. Luckily, we had no other customers at the time except for Old Joe, and he seemed to enjoy the action from the comfort of his armchair.

The scuffle did not last long, and from my recent observations, pub fights appear to be nothing like a bar brawl in cowboy movies. In real life, they are much more scrappy affairs. People do not hit each other cleanly, fly balletically through the air or obligingly fall down when someone delivers a crisp haymaker. Thankfully, the average pub bounce-up seems not unlike a playground scuffle, with more pushing, shouting and wrestling than damaging blows exchanged. There are, of course, some really ugly pub fights, and many licensees live in constant fear of being attacked and badly injured. In my short time at the Leo I have been threatened several times, but the attacks have been mostly verbal, and those making them have been assisted off the premises and barred for the standard term of one hundred and one years.

The most irritating part of the scrimmage today came when I got between the protagonists, and they forgot their differences and turned on me. Though I suffered little physical wear and tear, I had a brand new shirt torn off my back and split the seat of my trousers. After getting them out of the pub and administering the usual ban, I went upstairs for sympathy but found my wife more angry about the damage to my clothes than sorry for the pain of my swollen knuckles and the damage to my dignity.

Wednesday 1st

Incredibly, I have had an official caution from the police, and it is touch and go whether I am to be charged with assault.

I was working in the cellar this afternoon when Dirty Barry came in to say that a police officer wanted to see me about the injuries caused to the two punch-up specialists I ejected this morning. At first and given the date, I thought it was a not very funny April Fool hoax, but when I arrived in the lounge I found a severe-looking uniformed woman waiting to give me a talking-to. She said that one of my two former customers had been to the station down the road to lodge a complaint that I had deliberately banged his head against the doorframe while ejecting him and his friend. The incident, he claimed, had so traumatised him it was unlikely that he would be able to bring himself to visit the Ship Leopard again. The policewoman also said my former customer said he had taken legal advice, and was considering suing me for compensation, and would lay charges against me if I did not make him a reasonable offer to cover his mental anguish.

The worst aspect of the whole affair was that, rather than sympathising with me and dismissing his ludicrous claims out of hand, the policewoman was obviously on the side of the real villains of the piece. When I protested, she explained that she was a new sort of police officer, trained to see both sides of any situation (as only a woman can), and that I had to realise that things were different nowadays. Burly licensees could no longer make a good living out of filling their customers with drink, then throwing them out on the street when it suited them. I had a responsibility to what she called the two casualties of the social system, who were not to blame for their background and upbringing. Would I, she asked, like her to bring them in to the pub and act as a negotiator while we explored our inner feelings and resolved our differences?

After sitting down for a moment, I explained carefully that, as far as I was concerned, her clients were a couple of degenerates who would certainly never be allowed in my pub again. Rather than acting as a negotiator, I thought she would be doing her job better if she concentrated on nabbing a few real villains and making the area a safer and better place in which to live and work for decent people. It being obvious that we were not going to see eye-to-eye on the way ahead for modern policing, I said I would vigorously defend any charges of wrongdoing, and returned to the cellar to relieve my feelings by kicking the nearest barrel of beer and shouting at Tyson for hiding when the trouble started.

One of the swamp creatures who started the fight over the pool table had the brass neck to come in today as if nothing had happened. He did not stay long enough for me to introduce him to the doorframe again, but his reappearance made me even more determined to change the whole culture of the public bar. Despite my attempts to create a homely atmosphere for honest working people, we still seem to be infested with the detritus of society. Their lives are obviously so unhappy that they wish to visit their grief on everyone else, and seem to delight in provoking trouble wherever they are. They come in all shapes and sizes, and the smaller versions are obviously easier to handle, but particularly good at egging their friends on to cause real trouble.

I find the most physically intimidating types are the specimens who enter the bar with a rolling swagger as they concentrate on placing one foot in front of the other. Like cormorants drying their wings after a dip, they then stand at the bar with heavily tattooed arms akimbo, toes turned out and head swaying rhythmically from side to side. When I first encountered one of these creatures, I didn't know whether to serve him a pint or throw him a fish.

According to my beginner's guide to psychology, most of the problems of confrontation and violence nowadays stem from what the author calls maladjusted social comparison, and that we have moved from being a collective society to an individualistic one. Whatever this means and whatever the reason, these thugs give me a nervous stomach and are not the sort of people I would ever want in my front room as guests.

The pool table is going.

* * * * *

Another deeply depressing session, unrelieved by a visit from our bank manager. Had I known he was dropping in, I would have sent Dirty Barry out to round up some passers-by and offer them free beer to come in and make the place look busy.

As it was, the guardian of our account arrived at just after noon to find the lounge bar emptier than the Gobi Desert on a particularly slow day. Putting on a brave face, I told him he had just missed a huge crowd of regulars who had gone on the weekly pub outing, but I don't think he believed me. He looked even unhappier than our accountant and the man from the brewery, and the way he went on you would have thought it was his own money at risk. When I brought this point up, he explained that, in fact, it was now the bank's money that we were playing with. We were already running an overdraft, and, having sold our house to raise the money for the ingoing costs, have no security other than the pub lease to put against our loans.

Looking around, he asked me if I honestly thought anyone else would pay what we had for the Ship Leopard. I protested that he was displaying an entirely different attitude than when we first went to see him with the idea of running a pub; at that meeting, he had seemed nearly as enthusiastic as me, and had actually said that he had often thought about the attractions of being a publican rather than a bank manager. He responded by reminding me that I had forecast a healthy profit right from the start of our occupancy of the Ship Leopard, yet almost all the transfers for the past month had been out rather than in to our account.

After another drink, he suggested a meeting in the bank at the end of next month. If things are no better by then, he said ominously, he would have to review the situation. For someone so concerned about our trading income, I noticed he did not offer to pay for the two large scotches he drank during our encounter.

Friday 10th

Another visitor arrived today to tell us how badly we are doing, but this one is sure he has all the answers to our problems. He is what is called a pub marketing consultant, recommended by our accountant and seconded by the bank manager as an offer of help we cannot afford to refuse if we wish to keep our overdraft going. The so-called expert exudes confidence with his after-shave, is what I would call a suited hooligan, and a perfect example of George Bernard Shaw's dictum about people who can't do something becoming teachers in the subject. This chap has never run a pub, but obviously finds it profitable to spend his time telling failed licensees what they are doing wrong. After flicking through our accounts and asking a few pertinent and several impertinent questions about our personal financial situation, the sort of customers we want to attract and the type of trade available in the area, he snapped his slimline briefcase shut with a flourish and departed, promising a solution within the week. I noticed he drives a brand new BMW, so if nothing else he must be good at persuading people his advice is worth taking.

Tuesday 14th

I received the recommendations from our marketing specialist this morning. It confirmed my suspicions about consultants charging fat fees to tell their customers what they already know.

In the flashy document, he used a lot of charts, graphs and technical terms while coming to the conclusion that our overheads are too high and our incomings too small. His suggestion is that we forget my ideas of recreating a traditional corner local and introducing quality catering. We should instead go baldheaded for something called the C2DE Youth Market. Basically this would involve getting rid of all my regulars over 25 years of age and actively encouraging visits from the sort of people I have been busily throwing out during the past two months. His proposals for filling the Leo to overflowing every night of the week include disco nights, wet tee-shirt contests and karaoke singalongs. He also suggested that we make an effort to attract more stag parties, and even put on Hen Nights with male strippers and 'himbo' barmen to encourage women visitors. As the *coup de grace*, he recommended not only keeping the pool table, but putting another one alongside it. I can only presume that this will be so there will be no waiting between fights. I also don't want to imagine what Deaf Dolly would look like in a wet tee-shirt, and what Dirty Barry wears beneath his eternal cardigan and grimy shirt does not bear thinking about.

I filed the pub pundit's report in the waste bin in my office and put the episode and cost down to experience. If nothing else, his bill for no more than a day's work demonstrated how he can afford to drive such a nice car, and he has obviously found the perfect way to make big money out of public houses without having to go to the trouble of owning or running one.

Friday 17th

I am worried about my wife. After closing time I tried to discuss the pool table situation and my plans for the improvements in the public bar, but she seemed utterly disinterested. All she said was that I obviously knew the best and quickest way to ruin us and our marriage, so her thoughts would be of little value. The night ended with a full-blown row and I slept in the spare room, while Tyson usurped my place in the marital bed. I could hear his drunken snores through the thin wall, and in between them my wife's quiet sobbing.

Saturday 18th

I have been totally stupid and self-centred. My wife and I made up our differences this morning after I took her flowers and breakfast in bed and said I was sorry for last night, for the past three months, and for that matter, the pain I had caused her in the past twenty five years. After looking at me for a moment, she started to cry, then let me hold her in my arms while she explained how much she loves me and how much she hates the pub and everything about it. She confessed that she can't bear parading herself behind the bar and has been physically sick every time she has gone on duty. She reminded me that she never wanted to have anything to do with running a pub, but said she would walk in hell to follow me. I love her so much, and yet I have given her the opposite of what she wants. One of a family of eight, my wife grew up in a tiny terraced two-bedroomed house in this city, and always dreamed of escaping to the countryside and keeping animals. Now I have brought her into a pub in the most densely occupied part of one of the most densely populated places in Britain. She has tried to be brave and supportive, and I have as usual failed to see how unhappy she has been while I have blundered along pursuing my own dreams. After laying together on the bed and reminding ourselves of the rocky straits we have navigated together, we reached a compromise. From now on, my wife will look after the books and all paperwork and need never come into the bars again. She is sure that I will do the right thing to bring the customers in and start showing a profit, but I have not told her we now have no more than a month to make a go of the Ship Leopard. If the worst happens, we could be out on the streets with no job or even a home. It is a well-known saying in the profession that a renting landlord arrives at and leaves his pub with no more than a suitcase, so it is important that the case be stuffed with money. If we lose the Leo, we will be travelling into an uncertain future with very little luggage.

*   *   *   *   *

As we talked about my ideas for the flowering of the Ship Leopard, I promised my wife that, when trade gets better, we will look for a new home of our own. It will be somewhere buried in the countryside where we can escape for long weekends when Dirty Barry is fit to be left in charge. It is important that we get back on to the property ladder, and if we find the right rural hideaway, it will be an idyllic place for our retirement. I shall have to plunge us into even more debt to raise the deposit, but hopefully property prices will increase in the coming years and give us some equity and security.

Thursday 23rd

Disastrous news on the home front. I looked at some details of properties in the rural areas of Hampshire and discovered that a ruined barn for conversion is now valued at more than twice the price of the five-bedroomed town house we sold less than a year ago to fund the pub project. Realising we would have to lower our sights, I phoned the local estate agent about an empty house in the street alongside the Leopard. It is a dilapidated little box, but I thought we would be able to rent it out to cover the mortgage and clamber back on to the lowest rung of the house-owning ladder. When I heard the asking price and told the agent that I just wanted to buy one house and not the entire terrace, he haughtily asked if I had been out of the country for the past few months, or had somehow not heard how much property prices have soared in that time. For good measure he added that the house was actually a real bargain, as it was in a poor state of repair. Normally, it would be a disadvantage to live so near licensed premises, but he assured me that the pub on the corner was a total failure and had hardly any customers, so I would not need to worry about noise problems.

Friday 24th

Another two customers barred for life from the public bar today, pushing the tally for the month into double figures. Tez the Prez says he admires my spirit, and that I must hold some sort of publican's record for chucking people out rather than persuading them to come in. I know he and the rest of the landlords in the area think I am demented, but I will not lower my standards. This morning a weird creature stumbled through the doors and eventually managed to ask for the use of the cigarette lighter refill cylinder I keep behind the bar. While I served another customer, he disappeared in the direction of the toilets and that was the last I saw of him. Later I found the empty gas cylinder in the toilet cubicle, and Dirty Barry said he saw the user float out of the bar with a contented smile on his face. I don't know if he is a pot smoker as well as substance abuser, but with the amount of gas he consumed he would be most unwise to light a joint for a day or so.

Monday 27th

The pool table has gone. There were the predictable howls of complaint and we have lost some of the regulars, but I can't say I am sorry to see them leave. The trouble is that I have nobody to replace them until I refurbish the public bar and introduce my catering services. We have also had a solemn deputation from the men's and ladies' pool teams who have threatened that they will boycott the Leo if I do not put the table back. Their spokesman was Spare Parts Paddy, the captain of the men's team and someone who seems intent on leaving this world by stealth. He is not a well man, and when not in the Leo practicing on the pool table, he is on an operating table letting surgeons practice on him while having various non-vital organs removed. Despite the constant reduction of his bodily parts, Paddy bears his losses with fortitude. His partner is Long Molly, who is captain of the ladies' pool team, and she is as robust as he is fragile. She is fiercely protective of him and it is alleged she has a tattoo on her right buttock with a heart above his name and a list of the internal organs her loved one has lost since they have been together. They make an odd but obviously contented and loving pair and I shall be very sorry to see them go. Perhaps Paddy will give me the leftovers from his next trip to St James' hospital, and I will frame them above the bar so that at least some part of him will remain forever at his former local.

Tuesday 28th

To try and engender some spirit and enthusiasm amongst the regulars I have started a Christmas Club.
A sadly long-departed pub tradition, the premise is that the

customers put aside a few pounds every week to provide some extra spending money during the festive period. In theory, the deduction straight from the husband's pay packet was to pay for luxury food items and presents for the family. In practice it usually came out of the pub strongbox on shareout day and straight back into the till.

The pub Christmas Club reached its heyday in the early 1960s, then lost favour with the changeover to wages being paid by cheque rather than in cash. The tendency for the club secretary to run off with the money and the barmaid in early December also affected the decline. Nowadays, credit facilities for the working classes have made the pub savings club scheme redundant. Invariably, it is a case of putting Christmas on the plastic and worrying about paying for it later, which is another reason the early months of the year are so bad in the licensed profession. But the idea of a traditional thrift club appeals to me, and I am hoping it will attract a few more customers on pay day. Another function of the Christmas Club was to provide a fund for customers to borrow against in lean times, but people were much more willing to play by the rules then, and I shall not be offering that service.

I have learned much about lending money to customers in the relatively short time I have been a licensee, and it has been a costly experience. Apart from the risk factor of never seeing the money or the customer again, I have found that the most irritating aspect of advancing credit regularly is that the time between lending and borrowing becomes increasingly shorter. One particular customer would borrow a twenty pound note from me each Monday evening, then settle his debt on the following Friday when his wages arrived. After some weeks of this system working well, he began to delay repayment until a day or two later. Eventually, he was settling the debt early each Monday evening, then borrowing the same amount back well before closing time. Sometimes and just for the fun of it, I would mark the note he gave me to be sure he got exactly the same one back. After a month or so and with the weekly repayment threatening to come after he had borrowed the next installment, I began to lose track of who the note belonged to and how much he owed me at any time, so devised a plan. When he settled up next time, I put the money in a glass jar on the shelf behind the bar as I explained the new rules. The note, I said, was now his. Rather than borrow from me and repay it each week, all he had to do was ask for the glass jar when he needed it, then replace the note when he was flush. The only condition was that he could never ask me for another loan. Predictably, after a few toings-and-froings, the jar now remains resolutely empty.

Thursday 30th

A suitable end to a dismal month, as the Ship Leopard is now officially cursed. A swarthy woman pretending to be a Romany came in this morning, trying to sell sprigs of lucky heather to the handful of regulars on duty. Predictably, she was out of luck, and Mad Max, who is one of my more shady general dealer customers, tried to sell her what he said was a genuine crystal ball once belonging to the original Gypsy Rose Lee. I know he has at least a hundred of them in his van, and as each contains a miniature cottage which becomes covered with snow when shaken, I could see she was not impressed. To cheer her up, I gave her a pound for two measly sprays of the heather, when she immediately grasped my hand and insisted on giving me a character reading. Glaring round at my customers, she said that she could see I was a good man, but far too generous. To succeed in life, I would have to be much more careful with my money, and not let people take advantage of me.

She then stuck out her own palm, and when I tried to give her another pound, she said that the reading was worth much more, and a fair 'gift' would be at least ten pounds. When I refused and cited her caution that I should be more careful with my money, she became outraged, called down a curse on me, my pub and everyone who ever uses it in the future, and stormed out. The way things are at the moment, I do not see how a curse can make things any worse, and perhaps the heather will even bring me luck.

Always a Warm Welcome

The traditional use of 'governor' when referring to a pub host was not always a term of respect. In the early 19th century, many licensees were notorious for 'governing' their pubs by bullying their customers, taking all their money and then throwing them out on to the street. The use of 'landlord' for all publicans came about as a result of the first proper public houses being owned by the local landowner, who was often also a lord. This explains why many country pub signs bear coats of arms. The signs were to declare the ownership of the pub, and to warn any men-at-arms from neighbouring estates that they would not get a particularly warm welcome from any local squaddies inside at the time…

70

MAY

No sign of Spring, the weather is awful and the hard times continue. Our financial situation is becoming truly desperate, and I am certain we have no more than a month to start showing a profit before the bank manager pulls the plug. Apart from that, things are not too bad. There is continuing and strong feeling in the public bar about the missing pool table, but I am determined to stand firm. It has become a symbol of my struggle to change the character of the Ship Leopard. Now the table has gone, I can forge ahead with my plans to upgrade the public bar and create a proper dining area with an imaginative but unchallenging menu.

At the moment, our food trade is virtually non-existent, and I have good reason to believe that some of the meat pies in the glass box on the counter have been there since before I took over at the Leo. According to the previous landlord, the regulars consider that eating should be confined to the privacy of the home, and that money spent on food in pubs is a complete indulgence and waste.

But all the statistics show that food in pubs is a growth market and the way ahead for the industry in general, and I believe for the Ship Leopard in particular. Those licensees who do not adapt to take advantage of the huge potential for pub catering will not survive. I of course realise that I must not try to impose my tastes on my customers, or create too much of a culture shock by turning the public bar into some sort of pretentious bistro. Gastro-pubs are all the rage now, but I won't be trying to persuade my regulars to explore the delights of Japanese sushi or Indonesian batwing curry. I shall advance by stealth, starting with a simple but wholesome and value-for-money dish of the day, and progressing to more sophisticated offerings when I have started to attract the sort of customers who will appreciate them.

While I am about it, I will dispense with the rickety partition dividing the lounge from the public bar, which is a throwback to the days of more rigid class divisions. In Fothergill's time, all pubs had up to five separate bars, each used only by the appropriate level of customers. Labourers and ploughboys would down their pints of four ale in the public bar or taproom, while white-collar workers would ape their betters by drinking halves of bitter in the saloon, lounge or smoking room areas. In those simpler times, everyone knew his place, and stayed in it. Over the years, and as class barriers and distinctions became blurred, the walls of the various bars came down. The Ship Leopard is now the only pub along the strip with a separate public and lounge bar, with the different levels of comfort marked by an old carpet in the Lounge and a sheet of tattered and scarred linoleum in the Public. Although all customers get exactly the same drinks from the same taps, the previous landlord charged five pence more for a pint bought from the Lounge, and my regulars like to stay on their side of the partition.

I have kept the price differential in place as we need every penny, but it is a constant source of irritation to catch some especially mean regulars going in to the public bar to order and pay for their drink, then smuggling it back through the central toilets to enjoy the relative comforts of the Lounge.

Monday 3rd

Work is in full progress on the improvements, but I have been taken for another ride. A stranger with a crafty cockney accent appeared this morning and said he had heard I was looking for a carpet. He had just completed a job at a seafront hotel, and happened to have more than enough luxury deep-pile carpet left over to fit both the public and lounge bars. It would last for ever, and could be mine for a fraction of the proper price. When he assured me that his company had already been paid by the hotel for the full amount and it would only be thrown away if he took it back to the warehouse, I shook his hand and paid him in cash.

It was not till I and Dirty Barry unrolled the carpet that we found it had a fault running through it and two huge circular holes in the middle. I have put it down to yet more experience and the dart board mat will just about cover one of the damaged areas, but I am angry with myself for being so gullible.

Wednesday 12th

I have spent more money that we don't have, but I'm sure things will get better now the public bar of the Leo has had a significant makeover.

The public bar is transformed and now looks more like an Edwardian eating house than a thieves' kitchen. The holey carpet went down this morning and the walls are now a subtle shade of ochre. The customers are predictably suspicious, and show no interest so far in the offerings on the menu board, but I am sure I can win them over. We can't afford a chef at this stage, so I shall start the ball rolling with a few of my favourite recipes. My wife was out walking Tyson this morning when I decided to do a trial run, so I rooted around in the fridge and found a half-empty tin of peas and some prawns, and a chicken carcass that had been left on the worktop. Today's special will thus be George's Surprise Paella. The surprise will be that the dish will contain none of the more exotic ingredients usually found in the classic Spanish peasant dish, but I have plenty of rice to hand.

* * * * *

Not a single customer for my paella, or for anything else on the menu.. When I went outside to look for customers, I found what may have been a contributory factor. Someone has stolen my new menu board from the pavement, but I will not be beaten. I shall order a new one and a chain and padlock to go with it.

* * * * *

Spare Parts Paddy has been in to gloat. He told me that the Ship Leopard pool team has officially transferred to a pub down the road and that they are all very happy with the move. The table is more level and well-maintained, the team sandwiches are much better than ours, and the pub is packed every night. After inspecting my blackboard menu, he asked what paella is made of, and when I explained he sniffed and said he couldn't see me selling much foreign food in this area. As there are five Indian and two Thai restaurants, three Chinese takeaways and at least four kebab houses within a hundred yards of the Ship Leopard, I find his comment somewhat illogical.

Monday 17th

My first meeting as a fully paid-up member of the Licensed Victuallers Association this afternoon, and I was host. Officially the LVA is supposed to be a self-help organisation, but from what I have seen so far the members only seem interested in telling each other how much more beer they are selling than anyone else. But for all their talk, there is an air of desperation about them. Once upon a time there were more than a thousand licensed premises in the city, and it was said that there were more pubs than lamp posts in the notorious dockside area. With the biggest fleet in the world to entertain, gin palaces, cut-throat taverns, opium dens, riotous gambling houses and brothels stood shoulder to shoulder on mean cobbled streets where press gangs roamed and life was as cheap as a pint of rum. Now, the area is marginally more respectable, and there are fewer than one hundred and fifty real public houses in the whole city. Many rueful licensees say that this is still about a hundred too many. Membership of the LVA is dwindling and the meeting was heavy with an air of terminal gloom. Behind their watery smiles, most of my fellow publicans looked miserable, and the majority are obviously in a poor state of health. Curiously, they are either extremely overweight or apparently undernourished, and the trade curse of what they call 'galloping gout' seems endemic. I don't know where the image of the jolly, carefree mine host came from, but it was probably dreamed up by a shrewd 19th-century marketing man. It seems to me that most landlords have to be prepared to sacrifice their health for their business.

Apart from our president, the only licensee who was obviously happy with the level of trade was the landlord of the Black Dog. Without a thought for the sensibilities of his fellow members, Casser Blygh boasted that he could not fit in another customer unless they started hanging from the light fittings, and even made an insulting offer to send what he called his overflow down the road to me, who obviously needed all the trade I could get. He even offered to send his bouncers down to act as throwers-in, which raised a laugh at my expense.

* * * * *

We did not seem to do much business or pass any resolutions, but at least the LVA meeting allowed me to explain my plans and show off the improvements to the public bar. It was also a good way of getting rid of the vast mountain of unsold paella, which was too big for the fridge and has been sitting on the kitchen work surface upstairs all over the weekend. Spare Parts Paddy was obviously right with his prediction, and I have only sold one portion all week.

The solitary customer was a most uncivil civil servant who comes in occasionally, and claims he has a top-secret job testing naval weaponry during sea trials for new ships. He and his wife are near-alcoholics and spend his leave time touring the local pubs in a taxi and telling anyone who will listen how clever he is. I believe they come to the Leopard just to patronise me and laugh at my regulars. Yesterday he was topping-up his alcohol level before going away on another so-called secret mission, and ordered a dish of paella to show off his Spanish. After eating it with his mouth open and spitting bits of prawn shell into his beer and all over the bar, he told me I had used the wrong rice, and that the meal should have been served in the original cooking dish to be authentic. I told him it was a special regional recipe that had been handed down to my wife by her Castillian grandmother, but I don't think he believed me.

* * * * *

The LVA meeting broke up in mid-afternoon, but the landlord of the Black Dog returned with a couple of cronies to enjoy my misery during a deadly quiet evening session. He rubbed salt into the wound by saying he had to leave his own pub so as to make room for another three punters to get in and spend all their money.

After the last customers had gone, I locked up and went wearily upstairs to spend another restless night worrying about our future. Without turning on the light, I walked into the room above the public bar and looked out at the deserted strip. Hearing voices, I leaned forward and saw Casser Blygh standing in the pool of light from the lamp above our sign, and talking to one of my regulars. Flash Gordon is what licensees call a pub inspector, and his hobby is pedalling furiously along the strip, telling all the publicans what is happening in the other outlets. His vocabulary when describing the level of trade only seems to include 'deadly' or 'packed', and so he travels around, passing judgement on us all for the price of half a pint of mild.

As I watched, the landlord of the Black Dog reached out and patted him on the shoulder, then stood looking after the frail figure riding unsteadily away down the strip. Then, he turned to the wall, unzipped his fly and quite deliberately pissed on my front door. Though I knew that he could not see me, I instinctively backed away as he looked up at the darkened room before walking off in the direction of his own pub. I made a mental note to take a bucket of disinfectant to the spot first thing in the morning, and to keep a careful eye on Mr Casser Blygh. He has no reason to fear me as a competitor, but I think he would do me ill for no other reason than the pleasure it would give him.

Perhaps the pissing incident occurred because he had been

genuinely caught short, but his performance looked for all the world like a great ugly dog leaving his contemptuous mark on a rival's territory.

Tuesday 18th

A terrible night. I was in the toilet until dawn, voiding at each end. At first I thought I must have drunk a bad pint of beer the night before, but my wife said it was probably the paella. She told me she had put the chicken carcass I used on the worktop to remind her to throw it away, as even her stray cat had turned its nose up at it. Apart from my other concerns, I now have the anguish of worrying that I have poisoned the entire Licensed Victuallers Association, and my alcoholic civil servant has not been in since he tried a portion. I shall have to look in the evening paper for any news of a mystery bug raging through the city, or any sudden and mysterious rise in the death rate amongst local publicans.

*   *   *   *   *

Good news on the Portsmouth Pub Poisoning front. There were no reports in the local paper about the Licensed Victuallers Association being wiped out, though Flash Gordon the pub inspector arrived breathlessly this evening to say that Casser Blygh had not been seen all day, and that his barman had said he was upstairs with an upset stomach, being comforted by Juggsy the head barmaid. The drunken civil servant also came in, and was looking decidedly wan. He explained that he had been away at sea on a highly secret missile-testing mission immediately after his last visit to the Leo, but had gone down with a terrible case of vomiting and nausea on the first evening. So ill was he that the ship had to abandon the trials and turn back to port, which would cost the government millions and perhaps even endanger the security of the western world. The strange thing about the incident, he said, was that it was the first time in his career that he had been seasick, and conditions had been flat calm.

Trying to hide my relief, I bought him a drink in sympathy, and reminded him that even Nelson was a notoriously bad sailor.

Wednesday 19th

Not a good day. The rain continues and we desperately need a happening to persuade our customers to take shelter in the Leo. My wife remarked this evening that it is a pity we cannot celebrate Christmas all the year round, or find some other regular excuse for our customers to throw their money at us. Perhaps she is on to something. I shall retrieve the Christmas tree from the yard where my wife has planted it in an empty cask and put the decorations up again. I will also visit the library to check out the key celebratory dates of other major and minor world religions.

I do not think we have too many Bhuddists or Rosicrucians amongst our regular clientele, but I must find at least a tenuous excuse for staging regular and excessive drinking bouts at the Ship Leopard.

Thursday 20th

Another catering disaster. What the locals don't seem to understand is that I am not trying to introduce some middle-class gourmet's pantry into the public bar. In past centuries, oysters were the poor's staple diet, and working people ate out all the time simply because they could not afford a cooker at home. Today, we sold only two portions of my homemade chilli-con-carne and both customers complained that it tasted somehow gritty. I confronted my wife and she confessed that she had bought the cheapest mince for the dish as it seemed a waste to use best beef. When pressed, she admitted that she had actually bought the butcher's special line for animal members of the family, which was bound to contain a degree of crushed bone fragments.

We are, she reminded me, in dire financial straits, and if pet mince is good enough for Tyson, it is certainly good enough for the customers of the Ship Leopard.

Friday 28th

At last, things are definitely looking up. It seems that Spring has finally arrived and my wife has marked the first herald of summer by bedecking the fascia of the Ship Leopard with dozens of hanging baskets filled to overflowing with colourful flowers. A number have already been stolen by passers-by probably on their way to visit someone at the hospital at the end of the strip, but I have replaced them without telling my wife. Best of all, we have had a wonderful first Christmas behind bars.

After my wife's comments about giving our customers an excuse to drink, I declared a bonus Christmas at the Leo, and the exercise has certainly done wonders for the takings. To help create a festive ambience, I simply stuffed the juke box with seasonal music, put an advert in the paper, hung up some decorations, and offered a roast turkey lunch every day. I also persuaded Deaf Dolly to wear a sprig of holly behind her hearing aid, and Twiggy Bristols was very happy to wear a miniscule red outfit with a neckline that almost reached her navel. Even Dirty Barry got into the spirit of things and I heard him wishing several customers a grumpy season's greetings. Almost unbelievably, the customers not only enjoyed the stunt, but actually spent as if it were the real Christmas.

Even better, the fake New Year's Eve was a near-riot, with customers blocking off the street at midnight to link arms and tearfully sing *Auld Lang Syne* for the second time in five months. We have also enjoyed considerable publicity in the local newspaper, and a picture of our voluptuous barmaid dressed as Mother Christmas was splashed across the front page. We had some trouble from a fundamental Christian group who accused me of using their founder's name to make money, but I told them they should take my view that any publicity for their cause was good news. Another bonus for us is that the journalist who came to cover the story has adopted us as his local, and may be of future use in publicising the Ship Leopard. He says he likes the atmosphere, but I think Twiggy Bristols is the real attraction. He is also the journal's chief photographer, and is already discussing a golden future for her in glamour modelling.

My new press aide's name is Jason Eastwood and he is always broke and looking for ways to make some extra money, so his pub name will inevitably be Skint Eastwood. His particular forte is to dig up interesting local stories to send to contacts at national newspapers, who then pay him a fee for the tip-off, so I shall be very happy to help him earn lots of commission. He tells me that the tabloids he deals with are always interested in any unusual and preferably bizarre stories involving pubs, excessive drinking, sex or money scandals. I find this a sad commentary on the state of modern journalism and public taste, but the Leo should certainly provide a rich seam for Jason to mine, and some valuable publicity for us in the process.

Until the late Christmas stunt, I had not realised how easy it is to get free publicity, and my mind is afire with ideas for other suitable junkets. I have bought a book of worldwide celebrations and significant dates, and shall look for something to suit a promotion each month. I see that Tongan Independence Day is coming up, and then there's a choice between the Day of the Dead in Tibet and the anniversary of the invention of the spinning jenny.

For the first time in what seems a long time, I am feeling enthusiastic about my plans to make the Ship Leopard not only a classic corner local, but a financially successful one.

Saturday 29th

Another busy session, with a number of new faces appearing to look at our pub and what the tabloid press called the loony landlord. I shall leave the decorations in place, and I think I may just have stumbled on a way to entice more customers to the Ship Leopard.

Although I have a background in journalism, the idea of spoofing up stunts to attract media coverage and increase trade had not occurred to me before our second coming of Christmas. It seems ridiculous that people should visit a pub simply because a story about it has appeared in the media, but it obviously works now that celebrity is more important than old-fashioned virtues like ability or quality. I can't see the Leo being continually successful just through the extra custom created by publicity stunts, but once I have attracted new customers, it will be up to me to keep them. Since the upsurge in trade, I have dabbled with ideas for regular promotions based on anniversaries of historical events, but will have to be more selective with those I choose from the books I borrowed from the library.

Our Day of the Dead was not the lively event I had hoped for, and my planned celebration to mark the invention of the indelible pencil was a complete write-off. But most importantly, I have discovered that my regulars are all too willing to take any opportunity to drink too much if I come up with the right excuse, and I shall oblige them. The Late Christmas episode has also brought up a moral dilemma which never occurred to me when I was a civilian.

To be a real success, my job is to encourage as many people as possible to visit the Leo and give me lots of money while on the premises. Like a supermarket or any other retail business, spend per head is the key to maximum turnover and profit. But while I want my customers to spend well, I don't want them to drink too much for their own good, or to make a nuisance of themselves. This is one of the many unique challenges facing the licensee of a popular public house. In a supermarket, there is little chance that the customers will start a fight or make improper suggestions to the check-out girl if they buy too many packets of cornflakes. In an ideal situation my regulars would just give me all their spending money, and I would dole out the right amount of drinks for them every day.

On the theme of over-indulgence, I shall also have to watch my own consumption levels. Landlords have a reputation for drinking heavily, but civilian critics do not realise the amount of hours we spend on duty and how easy it is to drink a lot across an extended time span. Another perverse problem of the business is that licensees tend to drink too much when business is bad, and also when times are good. Apart from encouraging them to linger and spend more money, sharing a drink with one's customers is also a way to bear the more tedious moments. Most bank managers I know don't have to listen to a customer recounting the details of an exciting visit to the dentist or someone telling the same joke six times in one day. Consequently, I have found it all too easy to almost absent-mindedly get through several pints of Pompey Royal in the morning session and the same again at night. I have been trying to limit my drinking rate by adopting a half-pint glass, but one good swallow and it is time for a refill. Yesterday, my wife said she had asked Twiggy to keep count, and she said I got through eighteen halves of bitter in a single session. My wife has suggested I go on to soft drinks, but she does not understand my customers and their views on teetotal landlords. If they are expected to spend their money on drink when they visit a pub, they expect their landlord to set a fine example. I have noticed that if I abstain while they are in session, the members of my regular drinking colleges think I am somehow cheating.

I shall, however, have to take a more balanced approach to eating and drinking, as I am clearly putting on weight. It is a curious contradiction that my regulars who favour pints of stout seem to be almost cadaverously thin, but I believe this is because some of them do not actually eat solid foods and get all their calories from drink alone. My appetite, however, has not been deadened by increased drinking; in fact the opposite is true. Apart from a hearty breakfast and a few bar snacks during the day, I take a cooked lunch in mid-afternoon, and need a comforting supper as I wind down after closing time. We don't have a weighing machine, but after a particularly stinging taunt from a customer yesterday, I went to the chemist's shop over the road and got on their scales. The staff all crowded round and expressed amazement as the needle went off the scale, and one looked at a chart and said that to be the right weight for my height, I would need to be at least eight foot six inches tall.

I still feel healthy enough, but I am now having difficulty reaching the lower bottle shelves and it is proving to be a tight squeeze when Twiggy and I have reason to pass each other behind the bar. Perhaps I should think about going on a diet, but in the meantime I will make sure that my star barmaid serves anyone who wants a drink from a shelf below waist level. It will save on trouser buttons, and I am anyway sure that most of my regular male customers would rather see her bending over in front of them than me.

Public Health

In the 19th century, life expectancy was much shorter for everyone, and not helped by the prodigious consumption rates of most licensees and many of their customers. A medical survey of 1890 revealed that death as a direct result of drinking amongst publicans was nine times the national average...

JUNE

Despite the removal of the partition wall, my plans for the unification of the two bars have not worked out as intended. I can also see why the Public lacked a carpet, and it is now hard to tell the colour of the new one due to stains, cigarette burns and hundreds of blobs of rock-hard chewing gum. Strangely, even though there is now no physical barrier between the old lounge and public bars, the regulars have stayed on their side of the imaginary divide, eyeing each other suspiciously. According to yet another survey, we are now officially a classless society, but my customers clearly don't agree. The exception to the general apartheid comes when some of the meaner denizens of the lounge bar want to buy a drink, and step across the join in the carpets and on to old public bar territory. I have kept the price differential in place as a talking point, and rather than having to sneak through the toilets, my lounge bar regulars can now save money by simply crossing the line for a few minutes. Old Joe has even had his armchair moved so it straddles the divide, and by reaching across with his empty glass can order and pay in the public bar, but drink his pints in the Lounge. Further confusion is caused when Twiggy Bristols moves from one area to another while serving, and her admirers cross from one price zone to another in hot pursuit. The situation will be resolved tomorrow, as with the blossoming of trade in the past month, I now feel confident enough to put the prices up.

Tuesday 9th

A confrontational day, and most of my aged regulars have gone into shock. Early this morning, we spent an hour changing the sticky labels on all pumps and bottles, and generally hiked the price of all drinks by a few pence. In my times as a pub visitor, I never particularly noticed or worried about any fluctuations in the cost of a pint of beer, but to my older regulars it seems to be the most important thing in their lives. In some cases, the reaction has been so dramatic you would think they were auditioning for a part in a Shakespearean tragedy.

When Gordon the pub inspector came in and laid the exact money for his half pint of mild on the counter, I served it up and casually mentioned that he owed me another ten pence. After staring at me incredulously, he winced and stepped back as if I had made an indecent proposal, then eventually rummaged through his pockets, took out a coin and threw it dramatically on the counter. Having made his drink last even longer than the standard half hour, he donned his cycle clips in a most offensive manner and bid the rest of the customers farewell as if he were Captain Oates going out of the tent for the last time.

Other reactions from regulars who only ever buy themselves a drink have ranged from shock, disbelief and horror to actual accusations of profiteering. I am also becoming annoyed at their attempts at the stage whispers, heavy irony and enquiries about when we are taking our world cruises this year. It is a general rule of pubbery that all customers are convinced that every penny going in the till is bound straight for the licensee's pockets, and that he pays nothing for the drinks he sells. My customers also seem to think that making a financial return from working a hundred hours a week on either side of the bar is somehow immoral, while it is perfectly in order for a spoiled brat to earn a couple of million pounds a year for kicking a football about.

*   *   *   *   *

The price rise has cost me a regular customer, who officially resigned after I refused to give him a special disabled pensioner's discount. He dresses like a tramp, always pays for his drink in small change from what looks like a padlocked purse, and makes even my most tight-fisted customers look positively open-handed.

I considered calling an ambulance when I saw his face after telling him his pint had gone up by a few pence. The regulars say he is actually a property millionaire who owns more than fifty houses in the city, but is known to his tenants as Spooky because he is so mean that, if he were a ghost, he would refuse to give anyone a fright.

Thursday 11th

I saw the proprietor of the Black Dog today. It is delivery day, and as I was putting the empty barrels and crates out on the pavement ready for collection, Casser Blygh drove slowly past in a brand new Jaguar. He did not acknowledge me, but I could see he was making a close study of my returns. When the draymen saw him, they told me it is not uncommon practice for landlords to spy on other premises on delivery day, counting the empties to see what sort of week their rivals have had. I have obviously got Mr Blygh worried, and will trade on his fears.

Fortified by their cup of tea and bacon sandwich, the bemused draymen departed after putting my empty barrels back in the cellar. Next week, I shall have a mountain of empties on show outside the Leopard.

*   *   *   *   *

I am concerned about the cash register. After only giving the vaguest of indications as to the amount of money in the drawers at the end of every session since we arrived at the Leo, the figure on the paper till roll has agreed almost exactly with the contents nearly every day for more than a month. I phoned Big Tez and he says that a precisely balancing cash register is highly suspicious and very worrying. He suggested that I take a ten pound note out of the till when no members of staff are watching. If the balance is right at the end of the day's trading, someone is on the fiddle. I can't believe my staff would steal from me, but I suppose I must put them to the test.

Friday 12th

A little bonus earlier today when I topped up our catering supplies. I have virtually given up on the idea of establishing any sort of quality catering service in the Public, but with the increased business we are shifting a remarkable amount of snacks every week. Just as I was about to make my weekly phone order, a van driver arrived during the lunchtime session and explained he brought twice as many boxes of crisps from the depot as he needed for the round and had been told by his bosses to dispose of them before returning. He could let me have them for less than half the normal wholesale price, providing I paid him in cash. Following my experience with the carpet crook, I was determined not to be taken for a ride again, but he opened a box on the spot and invited me to try the goods. After a most enjoyable haggle, I beat him down to a quarter of the asking price for fifty boxes of assorted flavours.

When money had changed hands, he showed due respect for my bargaining prowess by standing me a drink and offering to personally load the cartons into the bottle store.

*   *   *   *   *

Bloody spivs. I visited the store this afternoon and discovered I have been had yet again. Rather than a range of flavours, all the boxes of crisps are essence of hedgehog, which was brought out as a promotional gimmick more than a year ago. Even worse, the stamps on the boxes say they are well past their sell-by date. Dirty Barry chose this moment to warn me that a plague of shady van drivers are said to be visiting local pubs to unload their dodgy goods. The result of my latest encounter with a travelling conman is that I now have at least a year's supply of stale crisps in one redundant flavour. Perhaps I will stage a gypsy campfire singalong promotion in the bottle yard next week.

Monday 15th

There is a spring in my step as I open the doors to welcome the week and the first droves of paying customers. We are now consistently busy with a broad spectrum of trade and the cash register is, if not approaching meltdown, at least pleasantly warm.

We are also gaining a reputation as what is known as a character pub, and I shall do everything to build on my reputation as a total eccentric. People can choose any public house to spend their money in, but seem attracted to the Leo now that there is something happening every week. I am sure many of the locals think I am mad, but if that is the price of success, I am happy to pay it. All my stunts and the attendant publicity thanks to my press agent Skint Eastwood are helping to build trade, and in the process upset my rival at the Black Dog. I feel we are settling in to a rhythm now, and my wife is happy with her project for turning the Ship Leopard into a country pub in town.

She has told me of her plans to convert the bottle yard into a beer garden, and I am content to let her go ahead. Whether the locals will take to sitting outside while enjoying the views of a whitewashed wall and stacks of empty beer crates is debatable, but it will give her an interest. I am a happy man, and all is well in our small world except my continuing weight gain. My plan for getting rid of the stale hedgehog crisps by eating them myself has not helped, and I am looking more and more like a caricature of a publican. To accommodate my new girth, I have taken to wearing outsize trousers with braces to keep them and my huge paunch in place.

My wife is clearly concerned with my ever-increasing waistline, but I know the customers like to see a well-rounded and happy host, and I am becoming a walking advertisement for the products of the Ship Leopard.

Friday 19th

The pool table is back. Now that all the swamp creatures and assorted non-humans who used to plague the Leo have been barred for life and beyond, I feel I can afford to relent. Besides, I have to accept that it brings in more each week than any dining table. The accountant, area manager and the bank manager will be nearly as happy as Spare Parts Paddy.

Saturday 20th

The Gents toilet door has been on its travels again. It arrived home with a policeman regular who said it had been found outside the station in the early hours and immediately taken into custody. Propping the errant fixture against the bar, the arresting officer told me that he and his Criminal Investigation Department were happy to bail it out to me on condition of its future good behaviour. Bringing it back had also given him a good excuse to drop in for a swift half.

Many licensees would not like the idea of having a police station on their doorstep, but I am more than happy to have the more sociable of the inmates as neighbours and regular customers. We were adopted by the plain clothes division of the local force shortly after Twiggy Bristols starred on the front page of the evening paper, and the Leo has become their home from home ever since.

When they first arrived just after I had rung the bell to signal the end of the lunchtime session, the mostly villainous-looking bunch of detectives were outraged when I observed the licensing laws and refused to serve them. After protracted negotiations had broken down, their leader said he would in that case simply stand at the bar and wait till opening time came round again. When we had glared at each other for a few moments, I said he was welcome to stay, and asked him if he would like a drink while he waited. Now, the plainclothes department from the local station are daily visitors. Their sergeant is a huge and fortunately gentle-natured man known rather predictably as El Sid. He is nearing retirement age and has been a sergeant for many years, though his colleagues say he could have done much better, but is a real policeman and has not progressed up the ladder because he prefers catching villains to playing politics and winning promotion.

Apart from their value in helping frighten off the local pond life and the prodigious amount of beer the squad shift each week, I genuinely enjoy the company of plainclothes policemen. In a way, they are not unlike publicans, as they work unsociable hours and have to deal with the worst aspects of humanity. No doubt because of this, they are generally philosophical, seem totally unshockable and share a sometimes grisly sense of humour. Last week, my first telephone call of the morning was from someone asking for the Murder Room, and he did not seem at all surprised when I told him he had come through to the Ship Leopard. When I asked El Sid about it, he said quite casually that they had left my number on the incident board at the police station as they were dealing with the murder of a prostitute in the docks area, and needed a reliable and convenient contact number while they were working on the case. As he and his team spent so much time in the Leo nowadays, my pub was obviously a far better base for investigation into the slaying. With my permission, one of his team would set up a blackboard and a few photographs of the murdered woman in the bottle store, then they would hardly need to report back to their official headquarters at all.

Another advantage of being the CID local is that they keep off-duty uniformed officers away from the Leo. I hope I am not a snob, but I don't want to encourage what my detective regulars call the woodentops. They don't seem to have the same spirit of unity as the plainclothes officers, and most of them plainly don't like publicans. Perhaps understandably, ordinary policemen see my profession as the cause of most of the trouble they have to clear up when the pubs empty at night. We get a regular visit from the uniformed sergeant responsible for the pubs in this area, and he is a pleasant enough fellow. He has started coming in towards the end of his shift, and I have set up a table and chair in the cellar so that we can talk business over a pint. I can tell he enjoys our little meetings, but he always insists on taking his helmet off before sitting down to his pint so he can officially declare himself off duty.

It was he who first interviewed me when I applied for the licence to see if I was a fit and proper person to be in charge of a pub. On the advice of my solicitor, I did not tell him about some minor excesses that had brought me to the attention of the police during my sometimes wild youth, but it came out in court when I stood up for my provisional licence to run the Leo.

After giving me a dressing-down for not disclosing the murkier details of my past life, the magistrate granted my application with a warning that I should learn to control my temper and my fists. When I got to know him better, the sergeant said that, in his opinion, evidence of my ability to handle myself in a punch-up should have been a qualification rather than an obstacle to my holding the licence for any pub in the city – and especially the Ship Leopard.

Monday 22nd

Another vibrant session. The bank manager has taken to coming in to savour his free scotch and tell me he always knew I would make a success of 'our' little venture. The man from the brewery has not been in to see me for weeks, which I am told is a very good sign. We are making a healthy profit, and at this rate, I shall soon be able to buy my wife her home in the Hampshire countryside. Another boost for business is that groups of people from a whole range of professions and trades are choosing to meet regularly at the Leo. Monday is street traders day, with the marketeers celebrating success or drowning their sorrows after the weekend. They can be coarse and loud, but are always good spenders. Tuesday is the turn for the car-dealing fraternity to meet and complain how badly they are doing and what crooks their customers are. On Wednesday the lounge bar is full of senior citizens who have just drawn their pension, and on Thursday the Leo is the most popular meeting place on the strip for local gangs of building site workers celebrating their weekly cash payday.

I have developed and nurtured these various drinking schools, and learned how to keep them on the premises while they are spending freely. There is a vital point when any group of customers look at their empty glasses and decide to move on elsewhere or stay for another drink. It is at this time I have found the value of offering the most valuable groups a free drink. If they accept, they are bound to buy me one back, and with the right level of customer care and manipulation I will probably win their custom for the rest of the session.

The only problem is that I have to drink along with them as if every day is my day off. Whereas they will have their major session of the week then stagger off home, I need to stay on duty and be ready to entertain the next batch. My weekly consumption of Pompey Royal continues to grow with our takings, and I have given up even thinking about a diet. It's a hard life at times, but a vital part of my remit as a successful publican is to drink for a living.

Wednesday 24th

I have taken a new tack on the catering issue, and it has been an unqualified success.

The breakthrough came when I visited a friend who manages an upmarket waterside pub near the headquarters of an international computer company. Although barely past noon, the pub was packed with lean executives in designer suits, all wolfing down junk food like starving road diggers in a transport cafe. Rather than listing the usual trendy pub food to be found in this sort of posh establishment, the blackboard menu began with double cheeseburger and chips, and ended with chips and chips. When I asked my friend if this was not an unusual and limited selection of offerings for such a trendy pub, he smiled smugly and explained. Every evening his customers go home to wafer-thin wives and partners who feed them on meagre low-cholesterol meals before packing them off for a brisk jog. But my friend knows that his customers would secretly prefer to tuck into a bacon sandwich. From the moment he unveiled his chips-with-everything menu it was a runaway success. Like adulterers having a lunchtime affair with their secretaries, his customers now sneak down to the pub and top up on forbidden fruits before going home in the evening and pretending to relish the tofu salad. Last week I decided to try the same approach, and the Leo menu now comprises mostly of hugely greasy snacks that should qualify for a government health warning. The higher the cholesterol level, the better the smart-suited types from the nearby offices like it. I knew I had won the battle when our bank manager started visiting us every day for a giant submarine roll stuffed with crispy bacon, sausages and fried onions and egg.

An added bonus is that, if times at the Leo ever become hard again, I can threaten to expose his guilty secret to his wife unless he provides the necessary umbrella when it is actually needed.

Friday 26th

The mystery of Rock-Steady Eddie's balancing act has been solved at last. Eddie is probably the heaviest drinker in the pub in more ways than one, and deservedly a living legend amongst the other regulars. He could certainly drink for England, and sees off at least ten pints of my strongest bitter each session. But Eddie's particular claim to fame is that, whatever stage of intoxication he has reached, he never falls over. He is as regular as clockwork, coming in every evening two hours before closing time and is always the last to leave. His conversation is limited, but I gather he is a retired sailor who lives alone on the outskirts of the city. Although there are at least fifty pubs serving the same beer as ours much nearer to his home, he has paid us the compliment of choosing the Leo as his local.

What makes a local is a complex and, I should imagine, a peculiarly British phenomenon. Logically, a local should be a customer's nearest pub, but this is rarely the case. A customer might refer to his regular pub as his local even if it is on the other side of the town. He might call a particular pub a local because it is the nearest to where he lives, but only visit it a couple of times a week en route to his real local. To the publican, a customer might count as a local simply because he lives in the neighbourhood, or because he is a regular user of the pub. Thus, any customer may be a regular, both a regular and a local, or a local who is not a regular.

By these classifications, Rock-Steady Eddie is a very regular non-local regular local. His nightly habit is to book a taxi on arrival at the Leo, then concentrate on becoming insensible before it arrives. As last orders are called, he nods off at the bar, but always remains reasonably upright. By tradition, the taxi driver will arrive, we will wake Eddie up, and after he has prepared himself for the journey he will be assisted from the premises by as many people as it takes. Tonight, the taxi did not arrive, and I was left alone with the slumbering giant.

Deciding to make him comfortable while I called the taxi company, or in desperation the fire brigade, I came round the bar to try and shift him to Joe's armchair. Predictably, he was impossible to move from his slumped position across the bar top, but his immobility seemed to come from more than just his dead weight. Further investigation as I struggled to get a hold on his belt revealed the secret of Eddie's legendary staying power. At around waist level on the front of the bar where he always stands, I found a large and obviously sturdy coat hook, evidently put there by some past landlord for female customers to hang their bags on whilst sitting at the bar. Our champion's belt buckle was latched securely on to the hook, and he was more hanging than standing.

After unhooking him and getting him into Old Joe's armchair, I ordered another cab and decided not to reveal Rock-Steady Eddie's secret. What man with a soul would want to rend apart the stuff of legend?

Measure for Measure

The traditional British pub measure of a pint is in fact French, brought over along with so many other new-fangled ideas by William the Conqueror in 1066. The legal measure for a single tot of spirits served in an English pub is, for some unknown and suitably illogical reason, exactly one-sixth of a gill, or multiples thereof. In the glorious days when British sailors received a daily measure of rum to give them spirit and mask the awful taste of their food, the petty-officer elected by his peers to serve the grog ration was invariably the man with the biggest hands. When dipping into the rum barrel, he would make sure his thumb was inside the measuring jug, thus swindling the crew out of a small but significant measure of their rightful share. The proceeds would later be enjoyed by the officer and his cronies.

The most popular measure with the Victorian pubgoer was the 'swift', which was approximately one third of a pint. Though never seen in pubs nowadays, the small glass is thought to be the origin of the expression: 'Let's go down to the pub for a swift one...'

JULY

The sun is shining even on this unrighteous area of the inner city, and I like being a landlord.

After months of struggle, we are earning a good living out of our little pub, and I am enjoying playing my small but significant part in the lives of our locals and regulars. In past times, village life revolved around the pub and church, and the licensee and vicar were respected figures. Times have changed and anyway, this square mile of pubs, shops and side streets jammed with terraced houses could never reflect life in any real village. But it is good to be part of an identifiable community within an overcrowded city where people often don't know what their neighbours look like, let alone what goes on behind their front doors.

Over the months, I have also changed my opinion about the amount of gossiping and rumour-spreading that goes on in the Ship Leopard. People knowing and talking about each other's business may seem to be a distasteful aspect of any small community, but it can be a useful way of making sure that nobody need go without help, and nobody is allowed to step too far over the boundaries of acceptable behaviour. If a pensioner round the corner has a problem, someone will let me know and the good folk of the Leopard can be relied on to help. Amongst my regulars there are representatives of every trade and profession who can be persuaded to give of their spare time for a neighbour in need, and there are subtle means of letting people know that the way they are treating their children, partners or even pets is not acceptable.

There is a delicate balance between interfering in people's lives and stepping in when a word or deed can prevent serious problems building, and I relish the challenge of playing my part in keeping our little society in harmony with itself. For all that, we still have to suffer the intrusions of outsiders, and I would pay a pretty penny to find out who is regularly stealing my toilet door.

Saturday 4th

More good news on the publicity front. We are in all the local papers with a story which involves sex, money and drinking. As Skint Eastwood says, this means it is bound to be widely read. The latest stunt came about when one of my more erudite customers mentioned that ancient Amazonian warrior women had one breast bigger than the other because of the daily exercise of drawing their bows. Inspiration struck after a couple of pints with my press attaché, and I have persuaded Twiggy Bristols to go on strike.

The story fed to the media was that my head barmaid has refused to pull any more cask ale as she is becoming lopsided due to the constant pulling of the hand pumps to draw the beer up from the cellar. Within the week, the papers were full of pictures showing Twiggy with one hand suggestively encircled around a phallic pump handle and looking sorrowfully down at her enormous and allegedly uneven cleavage. She has even appeared on regional TV, and the women's interest reporter from the local radio station came in to interview her about her mental anguish. Visitors have been flocking in to see the evidence with their own eyes and make interesting and mostly indecent proposals about how the situation can be remedied.

Twiggy is loving the attention, and the only drawback is that the other members of staff are trying to get in on the act. It is rumoured amongst the locals that Deaf Dolly has offered to pose topless for the Golden Years section of the evening paper, while Desperate Anne has started writing a kiss 'n' tell book about her tragic times with her former husband. Even Dirty Barry has taken to wearing a bow tie and offering interviews to anyone who looks remotely like a journalist. However, I have heard from Flash Gordon the pub inspector that Casser Blygh is hopping mad at all the free publicity we have received, so am delighted at the overall result of our latest pub-licity wheeze.

Tuesday 7th

Someone has been playing jokes on me. The dray arrived this morning with only half my order, which was particularly annoying as we are in the midst of a heatwave. When I phoned the brewery, they claimed that I had called to cancel some barrels of lager because trade was so bad. My area manager says that such hoax calls are not uncommon, and that this one probably came from an embittered former customer. My man at the brewery has arranged an emergency delivery for tomorrow, and says that if it happens again, he will organise a code word so that they will know it is me when I call. I have my suspicions as to who is behind the dirty trick, and they were confirmed when Flash Gordon arrived to say he had come from the Black Dog, and the landlord had sent a message that he had heard of my problems and would gladly lend me a few barrels.

I sent Gordon pedalling back to say that we would manage, to thank him for his offer and to say how sorry I was that business must be bad if he could spare such a major percentage of his weekly stock. I shall bide my time, but two can play at his sort of game.

Monday 13th

Another satisfyingly busy if bizarre start to the week. Amongst our early visitors this morning was Mad Max, who works the nearby street market with a fascinating variety of what he claims to be surplus or bankrupt stock. Despite the heat, he was wearing a hugely fluorescent anorak, bobble hat and tinted goggles, and had daubed his face with brightly coloured suncream. When I light-heartedly asked him where his skis were, he said he did not want to look stupid, so had left them outside. At first I thought he was putting up with the obvious discomfort to display and promote a new line of merchandise, but after drinking a pint of iced lager straight down, he explained the situation. He had taken his wife on a surprise and first-time ski holiday earlier in the year, and she had been thoughtless enough to break her leg on their first outing to the nursery slopes. They had obviously had to come home immediately, and before he had even had a chance to try out his expensive new equipment. Having laid out hundreds of pounds for the specialist clothing and accessories, he was determined to get some good wear out of it.

It says much for the sort of people who regularly use The Ship Leopard that nobody remarked on or even seemed to notice Max's unusual appearance.

*   *   *   *   *

Later, our circle was joined by Tracey and Terry, a young licensee couple who run a very successful fun pub just along the strip. A nice enough person, he is somewhat coarse, and much given to tight trousers and large rings made from gold coins. He also bedecks his attractive wife liberally with golden trophies as if to demonstrate his success and status in the pub league. They are a racy couple and were obviously bursting to let me in on a secret. Then a non-regular customer asked me if we could make him a salad roll, and Terry could contain himself no longer.

While his wife visited the Ladies in a show of mock-modesty, he explained that they had become involved in what he called a bit of nonsense with a cucumber in the pub kitchen earlier that morning. After their encounter, he had disposed of it in the waste bin, then gone to the market to buy a replacement with the rest of the day's produce. Arriving back at lunchtime after stopping off at another local pub, he had apologised to his cook for holding up her preparation work in the kitchen. She had said she had already served three filled rolls and a pork pie special, and had been short of salad garnish, but had coped by using her initiative. After rooting round, she had found what was obviously yesterday's cucumber in the bin, and had used it to go with the daily supply of filled rolls. The cucumber was perfectly sound except for being a little tacky and limp, she said, and had even ticked him off for his wastefulness in throwing it away.

For the next hour, Terry had watched with fascination as his customers worked their way through the salad rolls on the counter. He could not, he explained, have removed the cucumber slices without arousing comment, and anyway, one of the diners had gone out of his way to compliment him on the new and particularly piquant salad dressing. Such had been the reaction, he was actually thinking of making Cucumber Relish a regular catering feature at the Sticky Wicket.

Thursday 16th

An excellent day despite the heat. Tonight we staged a charity pool match to raise funds to paint a local pensioner's house, and made a rule that the players and spectators must dress as members of the opposite sex. As expected, Spare Parts Paddy's league team won the match easily, with the Addams family runners-up. I still do not know the family's real name, but I can see why the regulars have given them their pub nickname. Each seems to have only one head, but they are a very strange bunch who work in the betting shop over the road and shamble in every evening to haunt the dark corner by the juke box. There are at least six in the tribe, and I can't work out who is married to whom. With his greasy black hair, deathly-white pallor and staring eyes, the father looks like he would rather drink blood than his usual pint of cider and orange juice. All the family and their wives and girlfriends have an air of the undead about them and I don't know if they are intermarried, but they all look and dress and even speak alike, and have their own version of the local patois. There was an embarrassing moment when our panel awarded the best drag outfit prize to one hulking member of the Addams family who actually turned out to be female, and Gloria our resident transvestite was clearly distressed because he was not even nominated for the award. He is a nice man, but his size and looks do not suit his hobby.

During the week he comes in from his job as Graham the gravedigger, and looks every inch the solid working man with his mud-stained donkey jacket, craggy features and one huge hand wrapped around a pint of bitter. At weekends and on special occasions, Graham becomes Gloria, and seems much more at ease as his alter ego. Our first meeting was a bit of a shock when I recognised him through the makeup, but now I have learned to adjust our relationship to suit his incarnation. He appreciates it when I flirt with Gloria, and has told me she feels safe in the Leo, and knows that I will protect her from the sort of people who taunt her in the street or in rough pubs like the Black Dog. In an intimate moment Graham told me he was married once, but his wife left him because he kept borrowing her clothes.

What made it worse was that a mutual friend told her that he looked better in them than she did.

Friday 17th

Another good session today and a visit from another candidate for my weird register. He got through a dozen small bottles of barley wine, which is the drink of choice for really serious topers. My new customer had the usual toasted face and ravaged looks of his kind, but did not try to touch me for money or threaten me with violence when he got to number six, which is the usual sequence of events with this sort of drinker.

He was particularly polite and well-spoken, and during our conversation he told me he is of independent means, though does occasional television work. He hinted that he comes from a very wealthy family, and was in the process of deciding in which part of the world he would spend Christmas. When he left, Dirty Barry told me that our new regular actually lives in a nearby hostel for vagrants, and is known locally as Mr Woolworths.

The story goes that he fell asleep in the toilets of a local branch some years ago on Christmas Eve, and woke to find himself locked in the store. Before he was released some days later, he had celebrated his solitary Christmas by working his way through half the stock in the off-licence section. After coming to the national attention through press and television reports, he fell into the hands of an ambulance-chasing solicitor, and tried to sue the company for false imprisonment and the trauma of missing a quiet Christmas with his loved ones. All the odds were that he was in for a big payout, said Barry, but his immediate thirst got the better of him and he allegedly settled on the courtroom steps for a selection of gift vouchers to trade in for barley wine at the Leo.

*   *   *   *   *

I am worried about my nearest neighbour. According to our other long-serving regulars, Old Tom has been using the Ship Leopard since before it was built. Living next door to the pub he is a local as well as a regular, lives alone, and comes in for a single glass of milk stout every morning and evening at precisely the same time. Like many of our older customers, he is a former sailor, but unlike most of my senior regulars is always scrupulously polite and well-turned out, despite losing his wife some years ago. He does not talk about her, but the regulars say they were married for more than 60 years, and were a devoted couple. Now, Tom is marking time until he joins her.

Our old sailor was missing for a couple of sessions at the end of last week, so I went along with some bottles of his favourite beer to check that all was well. Looking drawn and grey, he seemed embarrassed to find me on the doorstep, but invited me in to his neat little front room where we talked for an hour about his past life and times. He said that he had seen a dozen landlords come and go in the fifty years he had lived next door to the pub, and thought I would make the best one because he could tell I cared about the place and the people who used it.

When I left, he gave me a large envelope and asked if I would look after it. Back at the pub I put it away in the office, but could not resist having a look inside. Along with a number of photographs of him in uniform and on the decks of various ships, there was a package carefully wrapped in pink tissue paper. Inside was his marriage certificate, and a fading picture of Tom and his beautiful young wife on the steps of the city registry office. After sitting and looking at the photograph and thinking how quickly time passes, I promised myself that I would make the best of every day left to my wife and I, and to remember, as Old Joe always says at the end of each session, it really is much later than you think.

Monday 20th

My wife went out for a tray of eggs today and came back with a dozen chickens. I said I hadn't realised she had been away that long, but she missed my joke and said earnestly that with the price of eggs and the amount we are now getting through, her scheme will make sound financial sense. She concluded her argument by saying that in the old days, every pub would have had a few chickens scratching about in the yard, and we would have the freshest eggs in the business. I don't think the customers will notice the extra freshness by the time their eggs have been fried and covered in ketchup, and the cost of feeding poultry nowadays is hardly chickenfeed, but I did not object.

Although rarely entering the bar now, my wife is obviously enjoying pretending our town pub is a country inn. It is now hard to see the front of the pub for hanging baskets and window boxes afire with flowers. Old Joe complained about an imaginary greenfly in his beer yesterday, but I think he, like many of our regulars, is secretly pleased with what we are doing to make the Leo a local of which to be proud.

Wednesday 22nd

I was woken this morning by the cockerel that my wife neglected to tell me she had bought to keep her hens on their toes. Having started to turn the bottle yard into a barnyard, my wife has now suggested we should invest in a pair of guard geese. She says that the yard leads on to a flat roof which is an open invitation to burglars, and showed me some statistics about pub break-ins. Tyson, she has at last admitted, is useless as a guard dog, and is anyway in a near-coma every night after polishing off all the beer slops. Geese, she said, are also good layers, and used as far back as Roman times to warn of intruders. I said that the local environmental health officer might take a dim view of keeping a complete farmyard's worth of livestock on the premises, but we ended as ever with a compromise. She has agreed to scrap her plans for buying a pair of alpine goats, and has my permission to create a small and more manageable menagerie in the yard to attract the family trade.

Friday 24th

Flash Gordon has been in to say that Casser Blygh is furious that the Ship Leopard is becoming the most popular pub on the strip. Just to upset him, I have taken to following his example and writing each day's take on the blackboard above the bar, and Gordon says that we have taken more than Blygh's pub every day this week.

What he and Casser Blygh do not know is that I have my own spies, and have been adjusting the daily figure to ensure that it just beats that of the Dog. A petty gesture, perhaps, but anything that gets under my enemy's skin makes my day a little brighter, and my regulars seem pleased to know that their pub is now one of the most successful in the area. Since the blossoming of the Leo, I have seen the change in my locals, and I suppose I have changed too. Perhaps we have come to realise that we have a common purpose, and I know that I have at last been accepted as a proper guv'nor. As Old Joe said before leaving this evening, I came to make the Leo my pub, but the regulars have made me their landlord.

Saturday 25th

We had our first police raid tonight. Admittedly, we were serving well beyond licensing hours, but the lock-in to mark a special occasion is common practice in the neighbourhood, and our beat bobby invariably turns a blind eye if the noise level is kept down and no harm is being done. Tonight, though, we received a visitation from an officious police sergeant, two uniformed constables, and the policewoman who had given me a ticking off for my rough handling of the swamp creatures.

Unfortunately for them, they were outnumbered by half the CID department who were already on the premises, and the uniforms had interrupted the leaving party for their superintendant, who was wearing one of Gloria's long blonde wigs while singing *A Policeman's Lot is Not a Happy One*. After getting a dressing down for confusing licence with liberty, they were ordered to take a drink before performing their own party pieces.

Monday 27th

Trade is now so good that I have taken on another member of staff. His sole job is to collect empty glasses and generally keep the Leo shipshape during busy sessions, and he is ideally suited to the work. In his green fluffy cardigan and frilly apron, Wally Twinkle flits around on his toes, exchanging badinage with the customers and encouraging them to drink up or bugger off and haunt somewhere else. Unlike Dirty Barry, he can make the most outrageous remarks to customers without them taking offence.

Small and delicate with cherubic features and a halo of silver hair, Wally is well into his seventies and in retirement from his long and successful career as a male prostitute. In his and the Royal Navy's heyday, he claims he was famous throughout the world, but with fewer and fewer lusty seamen and more and more enthusiastic amateurs around the docks area, demand for his professional range of services dried up years ago. Besides, he says, growing back problems and arthritis meant he was not able to keep up the standards that had made him so popular with the customers. His tales of life along the strip after the War are fascinating, and he is one of the few people still alive to have known and worked with the legendary Pompey Lil. All local pubgoers over the age of fifty have heard her name, but I have never met anyone who claims to have met or done business with her. Over the decades, her reputation has grown, and stories abound of her exploits with admirals, visiting royalty and even entire ship's crews. Physical descriptions of Pompey Lil vary widely, but all agree that she had only one eye, the other being lost during a dispute with a bottle-wielding rival who tried to set up business on her patch and now lies forever on her back at the bottom of the harbour.

Wally tells me that, rather than a drawback, the empty socket became one of Lil's most popular assets, and many an outward-bound seafarer would take advantage of her offer to keep an eye out for his return.

Wednesday 29th

My latest publicity stunt has not added to the profits. After reading yet another uninformed article about the disgraceful cost of beer in pubs compared to fifty years ago, I phoned the local paper and declared I would sell my best bitter at 1940s prices to anyone presenting the currency of the era. The morning after the piece appeared in print, Old Joe stumped in with a sack of pre-decimal pennies and threepenny bits. Apart from drinking his fill for less than half a crown, I learned to my cost that he had set up a thriving business selling the old coins to other regulars so they could also drink at a profit.

Thursday 30th

Old Tom is dead. When he did not appear this morning, I went to his house but could not get a reply. I could see through the net curtain that he was sitting in an armchair in the front room, and called the police. The sergeant broke in, and we found him sitting quietly by the mantelpiece, immaculately dressed in the suit he wore in the wedding photograph, and on his lap were two wedding rings.

Friday 31st

I found out today that Tom has no living relatives and rented his house, so it is not likely there will be enough money for a proper funeral. Old Joe has suggested that we run a fund-raising event to see our regular and neighbour off in style, and quietly gave me a hundred pounds to start the ball rolling. The longer I am at the Leo, the more I am learning about people, and at times like today, I realise how little I really know about human nature.

Signs of the Times

The most popular three names for British public houses are The Red Lion, The Crown and The Royal Oak. Apart from identifying a past noble owner, royalty or a famous event or battle, many public houses like The Shipwrights or The Plumbers Arms were named after the trade of most of their regular customers. In naval ports, it was common to name a pub after a famous ship or victory at sea - preferably against the French. The name 'tavern' for a pub providing more than just beer comes from the Latin tabernae, or wine shop. Roman hosts advertised their presence on the high street by hanging a bunch of grapes over the door, while early British publicans displayed an ale-stick and bush outside their premises.

AUGUST

High summer, and apart from the exterior of the Leo now looking more like a florist's shop than a pub, there is little register of the change of seasons here in the inner city. The daily routine continues as we all move on together to where the next sharp slap from fate's seemingly careless hand will land us. Standing at the door with my bucket and mop early this morning, I reflected for a moment on some of the other great mysteries of life before sluicing down the pavement. Why, for instance, do all types and consistencies of vomit contain small pieces of carrot? And why do people spend so much money on exotic takeaways just to throw them on the ground before they get home?

Despite the unpleasantness of my early morning clean-up, I like this time of day as I feel our little community has reclaimed the streets from the creatures of the night, and that the air is full of promise for a brisk day's trading. Along the strip, little stirs, as most of the traditional outlets have been replaced by fast food shops, café bars, antique and porn shops, and even an establishment selling what its owners call vegetarian shoes. Their and my customers are still abed, and the trading cycle has become later and later in the day.

Just a generation ago, the street would by now have been alive with greengrocers, butchers and bakers laying out their wares, and customers looking for early bargains. Today, there is only a single convenience store which has to open even longer hours than the Ship Leopard to survive, and across the road another once-thriving little business is having its shop window bricked up to become a bijou 'town cottage'. I have seen photographs of the strip at Christmastime in Edwardian times, and the pavements were full with people, and shop windows hidden behind tiers of turkeys and mountains of fruit and vegetables. Perhaps I feel so at home in this modest thoroughfare because my roots are here. It is strange to think that my Royal Marine great-great grandfather lived in the side street alongside the Ship Leopard, went from there to serve in the Crimean War, and was given a gun carriage funeral around these roads when he died in 1927. It is more than likely that he would have used the Leo, and I wonder how he would feel to know that his descendant is now the guv'nor of his old local. I hope he would have been pleased with my small achievement, and to know that we were having a better life than him because of what his and later generations had to go through.

Bizarrely, I learned only recently that his wife became one of the city's first traffic accident casualties when she was run down outside the Leo by a drunken driver of a brewer's horse-drawn dray. This morning I watched as gleaming cars bearing sullen children and their over-protective mothers whizzed by, all of them cocooned in their own little worlds and concerns, never knowing or understanding how good their lives are in comparison to those who went before. The only real human contact I made in the street this morning was with two vagrants, a man and woman clinging to each other and the wreckage of their lives. They didn't ask but I gave them some money to ease my guilt. Bleary eyed after a night on the streets, they were obviously going to the next station of their daily pilgrimage from off-licence to bench and hostel. As ever, they were walking urgently as if late for an important appointment, with their heads down and clutching on to the inevitable plastic shopping bags. Perhaps they take comfort in pretending they have somewhere to go and something to do when they get there.

*   *   *   *   *

A quiet start to the morning, so time for more outrageous tales from Wally Twinkle about local pub life a half-century ago.

Today he told us about the golden era directly after the last war, when fleets from around the world would regularly arrive in port on goodwill visits. All the dockside publicans, prostitutes, pimps and confidence tricksters would have a better knowledge of foreign shipping movements than the harbour master, and pitched battles would be fought at the railway station between local girls and professionals making a special journey from London to cash in on the jamboree. American sailors were known as the best customers and tippers, and Canadians the most likely to start a fight, but everyone in the local hospitality supply chain could make a small fortune.

Due to the law of supply and demand, the price of even a knee-trembler in a dank alley soared during these happy times, and some world-famous artistes such as Pompey Lil, Big Fat Sylvie and Peter The Pouffe could only be engaged through an appointments system. Although there were up to thirty public houses in some infamous streets, they all flourished, and it was said that no sailor of any navy could take a pint of ale in each and reach the last port of call. From what Wally has told us, this was more to do with the distractions and perils on route than the strength of the beer. Peter the Pouffe's party trick of dropping his trousers and picking up a bottle of Old English Ale without using his hands was enough to make the hardiest three-badge stoker blanche, and Big Fat Sylvie was said to have a dimple in the back of her leg specially reserved for junior ratings.

Wally's way of attracting custom was to leave his false teeth in his pint when he went to the toilet. This had the double advantage of advertising a certain area of his services, and also dissuading anyone from supping his beer while he was gone. If Pompey Lil was in the same pub, however, she would often steal his thunder by removing his dentures from the glass and replacing them with her false eye to show that her alternative and highly unusual facility was on offer to those in the know.

Wednesday 5th

A rewarding morning in the cellar with Pete the Pipes, the brewery's specialist in all matters concerning the maintenance and nurturing of my barrelled beer. I enjoy his visits and working together in the engine room of the Leo, going through the rites and rituals with filters, spiles, bungs and chocks to ensure that the cask ale is in prime condition and the keg beer at its sparkling best. This is a part of the publican's working life that the customers do not see or generally appreciate. In the so-called 'good old days', all ale was real, and conditions and practices in many cellars meant that the beer often looked and even tasted like lukewarm Windsor soup.

In baking summers long before the days of air conditioning and automatic temperature control, I would watch my grandfather wrapping wet sacks around the barrels in an effort to keep the contents cool, while in a thunderstorm he would often stay up all night to nurse his stock and stop the beer from becoming vinegar. The economies of the day also meant that what was left in the glasses after closing often had to be put back into the barrels. Many a customer would pay for and drink the same beer more than twice, and few would know or care. Then came the wonder of pasteurised keg beer, tubs of which could be rolled down the ramp into the cellar, plugged immediately in to the system and served within minutes of its arrival from the brewery. The introduction of the new process proved a boon to publicans and their customers, and it now takes little skill or effort to present a perfect pint of keg lager or bitter.

While this is good news for all concerned, it has taken the romance away from any notion of the licensee as leather-aproned craftsman, and there are some misguided traditionalists who would see us locked away in the depths of the cellar, labouring night and day to keep our ales in mint condition.

As I emerged from one of my subterranean sessions last week, I encountered a pimpled youth with a clipboard, wispy beard and the unmistakeable air of someone else waiting to tell me how to run my pub. He confirmed my suspicions by announcing that he was assistant venue secretary for the local branch of the Real Ale Liberation Front, and was waiting to carry out an inspection to see if my pub was worthy of entry in their Good Beer guide.

Before investigating further, he said his organisation would be greatly disturbed at the range of what he called 'fizzy beer' pumps on my bar, and that he had been in three times in the last month to find me off the premises. As I should know, he and his colleagues liked to see their licensees in their proper place, which was on duty and looking after the beer and the interests of their customers. My ironic apologies for being at my grandmother's funeral during one of his visits and in hospital having a brain tumour removed when he last called were lost on him.

I did not like to try the hammer and nails routine, in case he took me at my word and carefully pinioned me to the floor so I would be sure to be in for his next inspection of the premises.

Sunday 9th

When my little group of real ale fascists arrived this morning to spend a blissful hour smacking their lips and discussing the finer points of the bouquet, head and clarity (or lack of it) of the Pompey Royal, I directed them into a roped-off section of the public bar. I thought they would flounce off in a huff when I explained that they were upsetting my lager-drinking customers with their constant sneers and patronising comments, but they are so puffed up with self-importance that they actually liked the idea of being coralled away from the common herd.

As my tame reporter Skint Eastwood arrived to cover the story, they pinned him in the corner and lectured him for over an hour while posing happily for photographs showing them gravely staring at their glasses and measuring the head of froth to the nearest millimetre.

But I shall have the last laugh now that my weekly real ale Connoisseur's Challenge is taking off. The proposition is that each of the RALF members pays a ten pound entry fee, then takes his turn to identify a number of exotic real ales I claim to have specially imported and put on tap for the day. When they have had their fill of snuffling, gargling, discussing the tell-tale nuances of each glass and finally written down their answers, I announce the winner and present him with a specially engraved pewter mug and a certificate.

What they do not realise is that all the alleged tastings of Old Glossop's Hearty Headbanger and Frinton's Owd and Royal Gutthumper come from the same plastic bucket in the bottle yard store. My only regret is that I can never tell them that they have been rhapsodising over eggcup-sized samples of my fizziest keg bitter, which has spent the afternoon warming up to the muggy temperature and flat lifelessness of their so-called real ale.

Thursday 13th

The Post office was busy again this morning, so I knew the public bar would be like a doctor's surgery. It is benefit day, and I found myself catering for an army of walking wounded, all proudly displaying a neck brace, splint, plaster cast or pair of crutches, and in some cases more than one of these badges declaring their inability to earn an honest living.

Most of my allegedly disabled regulars are in fact in much better condition and fitter than me, and Bill The Back was his usual agile self while stretching across the pool table to pot a long-distance ball. He has allegedly been suffering from a recurring spinal condition for the past twenty years, and is usually very careful to check who is around before leaping from his wheelchair, but of late I have noted that he is becoming over-confident and careless. Last week he fell into a heated argument with a younger regular about their relative physical prowess, and entered his name on the list for our team entry to the city marathon before remembering his crippling disability.

Monday 17th

A relatively quiet morning session. We are still taking twice as much as during the winter of my discontent, but trade is definitely down, there are many familiar faces missing, and we do not seem to be attracting any new customers. My resident Job's comforter took gloomy delight today in telling me that the summer months at the Leo are traditionally even quieter than in January and February. He said with grim relish that our younger regulars migrate to the seafront pubs where they can pretend to be visitors, enjoy the weather and the pretty girls, and get away from the dingy surroundings and long faces that they have to put up with for the rest of the year in the local pubs. Next would be the empty months of autumn while everyone stayed away to try and save some money for Christmas. Then, of course, it would be back to the hard times of January, February and March.

After he had cheered himself up by making me miserable and gone off to spread despair at his next port of call, I toyed with the idea of putting him on a retainer to haunt the seaside pubs and frighten my regulars back to the Leo.

Thinking positively, I know I must make a special effort to bring the really good times back home to our little pub. I try not to be greedy, but if the Leo is not packed to the doors every day, I begin to feel insecure.

Tuesday 18th

A quiet but pleasant evening, with me holding court amongst a good sprinkling of friends and regulars.

One of the subtler hallmarks of any corner pub is that every single session is different, and the composition and general mood of the customers can make or destroy the atmosphere. Sometimes the mood of the gathering can be affected by the landlord or even an individual customer. A sensitive landlord can detect these variations and try to manipulate them to his purpose, but it is a demanding and even draining activity. Perhaps it is best that so many licensees seem to be so insensitive, and thus immune to the ever-changing undercurrent in their pubs.

At weekends when the bars are full and the stag gangs are on the roam, I have found that it is mostly a case of keeping the lid on. Generally in these busiest of times, people seem to lose themselves in the anonymity of the crowd; most importantly, behaviour that would threaten or mar quieter times is mostly swallowed up and neutralised, except when a pack of really dedicated troublemakers intrudes upon our territory. The challenge at these times is to ensure that the regulars feel safe and unthreatened by strangers appearing beside the campfire. As the village elder, it unfortunately falls upon me to confront and try to solve the problem.

On more restrained weekday evenings, the gradual build-up of bodies in the bar also indicates what sort of night it will be. If the right people appear, gather and stay, I can imagine no pleasanter way to spend an evening, with the hum of steady conversation punctuated by the odd burst of laughter, the clink of glasses being regularly collected, washed and refilled, and the cash register clanging with rewarding frequency. It is at these times that I feel most at ease. My customers are enjoying themselves, my staff are too busy to get into or cause mischief, money is being made and I as landlord have helped bring about this happy situation. When it happens, the local pub has fulfilled its promise and true purpose, and I can think of nowhere which can match what it has to offer in so many ways to so many different people.

This evening we achieved the steady ebb and flow of trade that every local licensee seeks. The early shift of non-locals arrived on their way home from work to tell each other about the dreadful day they had endured, and tell me how lucky I am to be my own boss and to have found true freedom.

As they drank up and departed to discuss with their wives and partners how spiritually and financially rewarding it would be to own a pub, it was time for my regulars to filter in and take their place in the mosaic of a typical session at what some of my locals are now calling the Club Leo. In the public bar area, it would be talk of sport and sex and What I Would Do If I Won The Lottery, with Twiggy Bristols leaning over the bar to serve a pint and launch another erotic fantasy. Across the invisible divide in the Lounge, middle-aged couples would be quietly contemplating their glasses and their lives together, while around them young men and women would play their courting games with little thought of where it could or would lead. And in my small corner, I would be sitting and watching and thinking about all the people who have brought their fears and joys through my door for another few hours of escape from the world outside.

*   *   *   *   *

Tonight saw a full gathering in what my regulars now call listener's corner, with me in my usual position at the end of the bar, my back to the wall and a pint to hand. With the increase in my weight and the popularity of the Ship Leopard, I have taken to spending most of our opening hours on what many licensees would call the wrong side of the bar.

Every licensee has the choice of which side of the counter he operates, and both have their advantages. By working behind the bar, he can save on staff wages and escape the unwanted attention of a customer by pretending someone is waiting for service. He can also avoid buying any of his regulars a drink. By taking up his position on the leisure side, the licensee is better able to keep his eye on all the action, and can also encourage drinking schools to congregate around him.

This evening I was on duty to chair the session's main topics of debate, which were to include why our local football team is faring so badly, the folly of allowing women and Europe to rule us, and why time passes twice as quickly in pubs as anywhere else. Amongst the gathering, I was especially pleased to see two of my favourite customers and friends, little Wingco and Big Reg.

Like all interesting pub characters, Wingco has a fund of stories to tell about his life and past times, and whether they are true or not is hardly important. A diminutive figure always clad in the same stained blazer and a vaguely military tie, he claims to have seen considerable action in the Battle of Britain, and that his permanently trembling hands are a result of traumatic encounters above the green swards of Kent. Some of my ex-service customers say that Wingco spent the wartime years in a canteen in Catterick rather than the cockpit of a Spitfire, but are careful not to challenge his stirring tales when Big Reg is at his side. The original gentle

121

giant, Reg is fiercely protective of his little friend, and is always there to catch him when it is time for Wingco's nightly passing-out ceremony. They live platonically together in a seedy bedsit at the other end of the strip, and make some kind of a living from a window-cleaning round. As Wingco, despite his alleged wartime exploits, has no head for heights, it is Reg's job to mount the ladder and clean the windows, and Wingco's to collect the money, ring the chamois leather out and be optimistic about the future. They remind me of the two central characters in *Of Mice and Men* as the evening wears on and Wingco begins to tell his friend once again how they will one day run a fleet of vans and staff with military precision, and clean up in the window-cleaning game.

During this evening's session I advanced Wingco another twenty pounds against future services, and have now paid for at least a year's worth of window washing, but I like him and his true friend, and they are part of what makes the Leo a proper pub.

Monday 24th

A home match for the ladies' darts team, and I continued my education in the workings of the feminine mind.

After the match and when the other customers and staff have gone, I re-open and tend the bar for a traditional afters session, and am tolerated as long as I keep the drinks coming and my male opinions to myself. I don't know whether to be pleased or hurt that the women completely ignore my presence during these sessions, but it is a unique opportunity to learn what most occupies their minds and thoughts. With the exception of a couple of youngsters who need the excuse to escape from babies and husbands for the night, the team is made up of middle-aged wives of successful car dealers, general builders and market stallholders. After an evening of drinking and relaxing in similar company, they like to sit at the bar and talk with utter candour about their lives, and the shortcomings of their husbands. I know that most women don't believe it, but when most men gather, there is relatively little talk of sex, and even less of personal performance and experiences. Work, sport, TV and cars are invariably the more important topics. With my ladies, recurring themes are the total uselessness and lack of vitality of their men, the comparative sizes and peculiarities of their sexual organs and preferences, and their universal and revolting personal habits. In a few months I have learned more about these ladies' husbands than their doctors, and perhaps even their mothers.

I have also learned that women are by far the most pragmatic of the sexes, especially when they have reached a certain age and situation. For my unsentimental ladies, their personal winning post will be passed when the mortgage is paid off and the husband has obligingly died and left them still young enough to enjoy being free of the unappetising and stultifying presence of men, and particularly their dirty underpants.

Wednesday 26th

It is amazing what the media thinks the public finds interesting. I am to star in my own television series, and it is thanks to my ballooning weight.

Over the months, I have been finding it more and more difficult to squeeze by the staff on the rare occasions I am behind the bar, and last week a regular who is a carpenter in his spare time came up with the solution. After measuring me up, he cut a neat semi-circle from the inside of the bartop, and lined it with a strip of crushed velvet. Now I have my own personal lay-by, and it has caused a near-sensation. As my spin doctor Skint Eastwood pointed out, it is a quiet time for news, and the press have been delighted to have the source of another loony landlord story.

Barely a day has gone by without me being pictured in some newspaper with my corporation resting comfortably in the cut-out section of the bar as Twiggy Bristols wobbles by with a pint in each hand, each carefully held at nipple level. As is the way of these things, the press report has also provided a creative springboard for another section of the media. Yesterday, a producer with the local TV company came in to see me perform my little trick, and has made an offer I found impossible to refuse. The proposal is that I will be filmed in my lay-by, then go on the evening magazine programme for a live weigh-in. When a doctor has shocked everyone but me with the news of how grossly overweight I am, I must give a pledge to try and lose the necessary tonnage over a set time. Each week the cameras will follow me as I visit health farms and try various dieting regimes and other slimming methods, and I will be sponsored by viewers in aid of a worthwhile charity.

My producer has made a rough estimate that a loss of anywhere around five stones would make compulsive viewing, and I have agreed to try to oblige. Personally and given the temptations of my profession, I think it might be easier to lose such an amount by having a leg cut off.

Friday 28th

I am recovering from my first and last Licensed Victualler's Banquet and Ball. This annual gathering would not normally be my idea of a stimulating night out, but I felt obliged to support my friend, mentor and outgoing president of the association, Big Tez. The event was held in a suite at the end of the city's Victorian pier, with two hundred licensees and their guests done up in their finery and obviously determined to outshine the sparkling glass balls and garish décor of the Crystal Lounge. For five long hours, I found myself encased in a hired dinner jacket and frilly shirt at least two sizes too small, attempting to wade through a rib-sticking menu with a main course of steak and kidney pudding, mashed swede and potatoes. It also seemed that each time I raised my fork to my mouth, it was time to put it down and get to my feet as we toasted everyone from our President, the outgoing committee and officers, the caterers and our disc jockey for the evening, and finally Her Majesty The Queen and every member of her extended family.

At last, dinner was over and it was time to get down to the serious business of uninterrupted drinking so all the publicans could tell each other how many barrels of beer a week they claimed to be selling, and their wives could tell each other how much they had paid for their peacock-train dresses.

By two in the morning, I was ready for my bed, and the evening ended with an unpleasant encounter in the toilets. My arch-rival the licensee of the Black Dog was taking up at least two spaces at the urinal and as I squeezed in alongside him, he farted wetly, then sneered down at me as he zipped up. When I acknowledged him with a curt nod, he pursed his oddly pink and tiny lips into a humourless smile, paused as if he were going to say something, then brushed dismissively past to return to the ball.

After I had rescued my wife from the attentions of a drunken licensee with a bad wig, hare lip and a golden cummerbund, we escaped to the cool night air and walked hand-in-hand along the seafront and back to the Leo. As we passed The Black Dog, I thought about Casser Blygh and the dirty tricks I am sure he has been playing on me. Although my success can do his pub with its sort of rough trade no real harm, I know that he resents and even hates me, and will do all he can to make my first year behind bars my last.

The Name Game

Until 1066, England's national drink had two names. It was called ale by the Danes in the east, and beer by the Saxons in the west of the country. After the Norman Conquest, the Danish name went out of fashion, and beer was what you asked for in your local. In the 15th century, hops from Holland were added for their bitter flavour and preserving qualities, and the word 'ale' was revived to describe the new drink. All those centuries ago, the stage was also set for the first real ale bores to begin their endless arguments over which local brew was best...

SEPTEMBER

The summer is officially over, but the weather is still too hot for my liking. The lazy days roll by, and too many of my regulars are still enjoying the fleshpots of the seafront. I shall have to come up with some more good reasons for them to spend their time and money with me, and I have laid my plans.

One advantage of the continuing good weather is that my wife's menagerie is proving a great success with the family trade if not with our immediate neighbours. Apart from the chickens and the guard geese, the back yard is now home to a whole range of exotic fauna, and the latest addition to our safari park is a vast Vietnamese potbellied pig. It is a boar, which my wife has, for some reason, christened George.

*　　*　　*　　*　　*

Filming for my television series started today, so perhaps the docu-soap series about the fat publican trying to lose weight will do the trick and attract some new faces to the Leo. This morning, I was picked up in a chauffeur-driven car and whisked to the city university to be given a going-over by a professor who is a nutritional expert. For a man who is supposed to know all about healthy eating and living, he was in a very poor state. Tall and cadaverous with a sallow complexion, his breath was terrible and he had a severe case of dandruff to compliment his unfortunate skin condition.

While I stripped to my underwear, he told me that virtually everyone in the western world overeats, and his personal regime includes eating just one apple and drinking six pints of water every other day to purify his system. Obviously, he is eating the wrong sort of apples, but I thought it best not to attempt to give him any dietary advice at this early stage of our acquaintance.

After he had officially weighed me in and checked the scales in disbelief, he put me through a series of physical tests and seemed to become increasingly irritated as I sailed through them with little discomfort. For more than an hour, the TV crew filmed me from all angles as I pedalled furiously on static bicycle machines, climbed up and down stepladders and blew into an outsized hot water bottle. When the professor had curtly refused my request for a fag break, we sat at a desk and the producer got me to nod inanely for something called reaction shots while I was lectured about the perils of carrying too much weight and leading what he called a chronically unhealthy life style. I then had to make a full and frank confession of everything I ate and drank in an average day while the professor tapped away on a special calculating machine.

After reaching the total, he seemed genuinely astonished, and declared he had just come back from a research trip to Africa, where he had visited entire villages which took in fewer calories a day than me.

Friday 4th

I am sure someone is setting me up, and who that someone is. A small and somehow disconcertingly neat man carrying a briefcase in a very aggressive manner marched into the public bar this morning and demanded to see me. He reeked of officialdom, and announced himself as an Environmental Health Officer, there to inspect my premises immediately. I could tell from the number of different coloured pens in the breast pocket of his jacket that there was no point in trying to engage him in any sort of philosophical discussion about the current hysterical obsession with hygiene, so just invited him to do his worst. Like my gloomy professor from earlier in the week, he is obviously the sort of person who is always looking for bad news about the human race and its failings, and his tour of the Ship Leopard must have cheered him up no end. After poking about in the bars, cellar and kitchen for an hour, he reappeared to report with grim satisfaction that he had found more than fifty hazards to the wellbeing of my staff and customers.

My crimes against humanity ranged from the perils posed by a tiny rip in the lounge bar carpet to an out-of-date yoghurt in the fridge, and I could not help thinking that it was just as well he had not arrived earlier in the year, when my paella surprise was incubating nicely on the kitchen worktop. But though I thought I had got away with our encounter fairly lightly, much worse was to come.

As I promised him I would mend my ways and steered him toward the door, our cockerel decided to get some crowing practice in, and the whole of my wife's menagerie responded with a cacophony of grunts, barks, bleats and whinnies. With the horrified look of a vegetarian who has wandered into an abbatoir, he snatched the reddest pen from his breast pocket and made straight for the bottle yard.

*   *   *   *   *

When the bemused health inspector had recovered sufficiently from his visit to my wife's urban wildlife park, I asked him why, of all the pubs on his patch, he had chosen mine to investigate. He muttered something about being obliged to investigate any allegation, but would not tell me who made the malicious call. Pausing only to re-arrange his coloured pens and wipe something nasty off his shoe, he staggered off, shaking his head sadly and leaving me with a long list of improvements to our health, hygiene and safety standards, including the re-urbanisation of the bottle yard.

Monday 7th

Troubles were obviously destined to come at battalion strength this week. Just before opening time this morning, another small and briefcase-bearing cove pitched up on the doorstep. With his death's head looks, rimless steel glasses and slash of a mouth, he needed only a leather trench coat and duelling scar to look the part of a particularly sadistic Gestapo officer having a bad hair day, and he had even more pens in his top pocket than yesterday's representative of the People. Laying his case on the counter with a proprietory air, he revealed that he was from the Customs and Excise Department, then watched my face to savour the inevitable reaction. All licensees know that ever since their days of galloping along clifftops and shooting innocent fisherman just in case they were smugglers, the men from the Revenue have had more power than any other single government body, and less accountability than the Spanish Inquisition. My visitor had arrived to make what he said was a random check on the contents of my barrels and bottles, but made straight for my back shelf as if he knew exactly what he was looking for.

While he worked with his syringes and syphons and set little glass weights bobbing in samples from every bottle on display, I tried to make conversation by recalling how his job would have been done in the Middle Ages. Then, the local quality assurance man would arrive at the village tavern, pour a pint of the house's ale on to a handy wooden bench and sit on it. If his leather trews stuck to the bench and made standing up difficult, the beer was said to be of sufficient body. The method of testing stronger drinks was a little more complex, and much more spectacular. After mixing a small measure of spirit with an equal amount of water and a pinch of gunpowder, the pub inspector would apply a light. If the mixture exploded, the spirit was said to be proved. If not, it was deemed to be under-strength and the guilty licensee was on his way to the stocks.

Unfortunately, my historical anecdotes did little to distract him from his search, and he eventually found what he had so obviously been looking for. Tucked away on a top shelf was an innocent-looking bottle of gin which, he demonstrated with his little glass balls, was actually stronger in alcoholic content than it should have been. This could only mean that it was a continental spirit which someone had brought across the Channel and poured into a British-branded bottle to disguise its foreign origins. Perversely, I was guilty of attempting to give my customers more rather than less alcohol for their money, but my really serious crime was the evasion of import duty on the bottle. As he packed up his kit and looked up at the ceiling as if searching for a handy beam to throw a rope across, the man from the Revenue said I would be reported and could be charged with the offence if my 'excuse' did not satisfy the authorities. He added that it was quite possible I could lose my licence as a fit and proper person to run a public house, and therefore (this said with the grimmest of relish) my livelihood with it.

*   *   *   *   *

The mystery of the illegal gin bottle has been solved. I believe the architect of my present misfortune is my rival from the Black Dog, and his instrument was certainly Dirty Barry. The events of the day have also cleared up the matter of the fluctuations in the accuracy of my cash register.

When the staff came on duty for the lunchtime session, I told them about the visit from the Revenue and the likely outcome, and I could see from my manager's face that he was the cause of my problem. I invited him in to the cellar expecting a flurry of denials and protestation, but he broke down immediately and told me everything. He said he had bought the bottle from a regular at the Black Dog who works on the cross-Channel ferries, and makes a secondary income from supplying customers and dishonest local licensees with duty-free cut-price cigarettes, beer and spirits. In between sobs, my bars manager admitted that he has been buying bottles of spirits regularly to add to my stock. This, I know from Tez the Prez, is an old trick and one regularly employed by cheating barstaff to disguise their thieving from the till. By neglecting to key in a round or two on the cash register in any session, a dishonest worker can simply take the equivalent amount from the till when nobody is watching, and the money in the drawer will still tally with the reading for the day's takings.

This, however, is only a short-term measure, as the shortcomings are sure to be discovered when the monthly stocktaker's check of what had been bought and sold and how much should have been taken over the bar shows a discrepancy. By adding a bottle when necessary, the books can be balanced and the outgoings and incomings made to agree. Nobody will be any the wiser, and the crooked staff member can pocket the difference between what he has paid for the cheap bottle and the price it has reached when sold in measures across the counter.

For months now, I discovered, Barry has been topping-up my stock to balance the books. But, rather than trying to steal from me, he swore that he had been spending his own money to give me peace of mind. When I had arrived at the Ship Leopard he had not liked me, and was even happy when trade was bad. But, over the months, he had come to admire what I was trying to do and wanted to be part of it. I was one of the few people apart from his mother to show him kindness, and not to laugh at him and try to make him feel small. He was certain that the bad readings with the till were not evidence of dishonesty by the staff, but mere incompetence. As my bars manager, he had felt that the responsibility for the shortages were his, and it was his duty to make things right. He realised that I would probably sack him now I had learned the truth and was in trouble with the Customs and Excise, but he wanted me to know he had only done what he had done for me and our pub.

After we had sat in silence for a while, I gave him a quick hug and a cleaning cloth to dry his eyes and suggested we take another night out along the strip tonight. My bars manager may have bad breath and, as the regulars say, musical feet, but I believe his heart is in the right place.

Friday 11th

Grim tidings from the Leo's star member of staff today. My publicity stunts based on Twiggy Bristols' considerable assets have backfired, and she is leaving us. She told me this morning that she has been talent-spotted by a friend of Skint Eastwood who works on a national tabloid newspaper, and she is to become a professional glamour model. I will have to start looking for a suitable replacement, but it will not be easy to find another Twiggy Bristols.

Saturday 12th

An uneventful day, except for the loss of Lamp Post Alec. Alec is a small Scot with a gentle manner and a ferocious thirst. By day he works in the kitchens of an old folk's home, and he likes to spend his evenings in keen contention for a place on our Fall of the Month plaque.

When I first came to the Ship Leopard, I was alarmed at the ease and regularity with which some of the more hardened lounge bar drinkers would measure their length on the carpet, but came to accept the practice as long as my regular floor-divers did no damage to themselves or the furniture. After a while and as the Leo grew in reputation and popularity, I noticed that an air of overtly theatrical competition was creeping in, with the various exponents vying to outdo each other for style and general impact on the audience as well as the floor. Now, a whole variety of freestyle techniques are on show as the judging panel prepares to sit. Some more reserved contestants will go for a wilting and leisurely decline from a bar stool, arriving at the prone position in stages. Others opt for a dramatic and sudden collapse while standing at the bar, and especially when I am there to see their performance. This can be particularly unnerving if you are on the other side of the counter and move away momentarily to serve another customer, then turn back and find the person you have been talking to has dramatically vanished.

After some heated disputes about who had gone missing in action with the most panache during one session, I formalised the competition by fixing a brass plaque to the counter, and inviting a panel of experts to decide whose name should be added to the roll of honour each month. Before our celebrity chef became a regular customer, Wingco had long been the undisputed floor-diving champion at the Leopard, but of late his title has been under threat. Alec's pub name came about because, rather than expiring inside the Leo, he prefers the theatre of the outdoors. Having had what he insists is his last drink of the evening, his habit is to stagger through the doors and engineer a collision with the street light immediately outside. After a suitable period for recovery on the pavement, he will stagger back into the bar to recover by taking what he calls his Absolutely Bloody Final.

Last night the opening stages of his routine went as normal, but he did not make his promised return, and when we sent a search party he was nowhere to be found.

Sunday 13th

Lamp Post Alec has happily returned to the fold with a bandaged head and a tale to tell. Apparently, the bulb in the street light outside our door had failed last evening, and he had lost his bearings, missed contact and wandered off into the night. He had woken up on the seafront this morning, and his logical conclusion is that he was instinctively drawn to the row of flashing fairy lights on the ornate Victorian lamp standards running along the promenade and around the children's boating pool.

Monday 14th

It is time to activate my plan to win back our missing regulars and at the same time restore another traditional pub activity. We will stage an allcomers talent show, and the winners will be booked to provide the entertainment at a grand charity cabaret show. The evening will not only raise money for a good cause, but will mark Twiggy Bristols' departure, and, if successful, become a regular weekend feature. Before the days of sitting supinely in front of a television screen at home, people had to make their own amusements, and everybody would have a party turn. No more than a generation ago, it was a rare corner pub which did not have at least a piano singalong each weekend, and I am going to mine the hidden abilities of my customers and staff. I do not expect them to be of professional standards, but am sure we will uncover some engaging talents.

I made up some posters this morning, and the staff are as keen as some of the customers to take part. To my surprise, I have discovered that Deaf Dolly was an accomplished pianist in her youth, and she has offered to accompany the singing acts. I tactfully asked her how she will know which tune to play, but she says that her lip-reading skills will more than compensate for her hearing difficulties.

Saturday 19th

I have decided to take my wife on a surprise holiday. She has been untiring in her mission to transform the Ship Leopard into a country pub in town, but obviously needs a break. I have no doubts about her durability, but a complete change of scenery will do us both good. It is well known in the trade that the nature of the pub business inevitably puts strains on even the strongest of marriages, and the casualty rate is high. The classic scenario is said to involve the husband running off with a barmaid or becoming an alcoholic or both, or the wife running off with the man who delivers the pies or even a customer, and/or becoming an alcoholic. This is hopefully not a likely outcome for either of us, but a break will allow us to recharge our batteries and make plans for the Christmas period. This morning I booked a week at a hotel across the Channel in Normandy, so we will be getting right away from the Ship Leopard. I am a little nervous about leaving our pub entirely in the hands of Barry, but he is loyal and reliable, and this will further demonstrate my complete trust in him as my manager.

Sunday 20th

Last night's talent show was not a great success. My bars manager had appointed himself the master of ceremonies, and turned up with a plastic ukelele, fringed shirt, cowboy boots and ridiculous stetson to do what I took to be an impersonation of George Formby singing *The Lonesome Cowboy*. Desperate Anne fell out with Gloria the transvestite gravedigger because they both wanted to sing the same Shirley Bassey song, and Deaf Dolly's lip-reading skills are obviously not what she claimed them to be. Other bizarre novelty acts included Lamp Post Alec beating himself over the head with a tin tray while singing *I Belong to Glasgow*, and Wingco playing The *Dam Busters March* on a comb and paper and drinking a double whisky at the same time. Old Joe's contribution was to stand on the stage and drink a pint of Pompey Royal in under fifteen seconds while balancing on one leg, but as a disgruntled member of the audience pointed out, he was at an unfair advantage as he had just one leg to start with. The only entertainment which brought the audience to its feet was Twiggy Bristols, who performed what she called an adult version of the Shirley Temple classic, *The Good Ship Lollipop*.

I think I shall have to abandon my plans for using only home-grown talent for the gala cabaret night, and will advertise for some less unusual yet more professional entertainers.

Wednesday 23rd

What is it about pub singers? This morning I sat through a dozen performances of well-known songs and didn't recognise one of them. All of my would-be entertainers spoke perfectly normally, and one or two could at least carry a tune, but as soon as they launched into song they became completely unintelligible. The worst offender was a little man called Eric with a limp, an all-too-obvious wig, orange make-up and a frilly shirt open to the waist. He was also wearing a huge medallion, and when he started his impression of Tom Jones, it sounded as if he had swallowed it.

Sunday 27th

It is the morning after the charity gala, and we are still clearing up. Like the curate's egg, the show was only good in parts, but the event raised a lot of money and it was good to see the bars packed with happy customers again. Inspired by Twiggy Bristol's performance, Skint Eastwood has also proposed a publicity stunt which will mark her departure and at the same time find someone suitable to take her place. After telling me that his newspaper has turned down our carefully-worded advertisement for a new barperson *(No experience necessary but must be young and pretty and have really big tits)* as discriminatory, he suggested we issue a unique challenge to find someone who can measure up to Twiggy's stature and allure. I have agreed to his proposals, but this time I think even he may have gone too far.

Wednesday 30th

A bizzarre end to another month in my apprenticeship as a publican. Before I took over the Leo, I would not have believed that part of my future duties would be conducting job interviews by asking young women to place their bosoms in a greengrocer's scale.

The pub was predictably packed for the grand weigh-in, with customers standing on seats, tables and even the bar to watch as a succession of contestants lined up to register their qualifications for replacing Twiggy Bristols. I was amazed at the response to our poster campaign, and it was obvious that the applicants were enjoying the ceremony as much as the spectators. After a slight altercation when one of the entrants was found to have cheated by sewing lead fishing weights into her brassiere, the winner and soon-to-be new barmaid at the Ship Leopard romped home by over half a kilo. A striking redhead called Mandy, she more than measures up to Twiggy Bristols, and I know she will be popular with the customers. Mandy has never worked behind a bar and says her adding-up skills are non-existent, but I am sure her other assets will outweigh those initial disadvantages.

It is an uncomfortable thought that male pub customers still place so much value on simple sexual characteristics rather than character, personality or efficiency of service, but it is the way things are, and I cannot afford to try and live outside the real world. And to be honest, as my greengrocer and invigilator said after checking Mandy's contribution to the scales, you don't get too many of those to the pound.

Fun for all the Family

Pubs have always been a focal point for home-made entertainment, and adept at drawing customers through the door with the appeal of their serving-wenches. Eighteenth-century country inns would regularly stage 'grinning matches', with regulars competing to make the most bizarre face through the frame of a horse collar. Other sophisticated talent competitions involved whistling, the fastest or slowest smoking of a pipe, and even yawning. In 1661, the great diarist Samuel Pepys recorded a visit to a London tavern where one of the first ever pub quizzes was taking place, and remarked how much he enjoyed collecting forfeit kisses from the barmaids who came up with the wrong answers...

OCTOBER

Autumn is with us, and our first Christmas behind bars is on the horizon. Business is booming again now that the last of my absentee regulars have returned from their summer migration, and Mandy Melons has proved a popular replacement for Twiggy Bristols. Other good news arrived this morning when I learned that I am not to be charged over the incident with the foreign gin bottle, and my rival at the Black Dog has come up with no further dirty tricks to spoil my business. Perhaps he has given in and accepts that I am here to stay. I know I should be happy that the Ship Leopard is sailing in such untroubled waters, but feel somehow jaded by the unchanging routine of my life behind bars. I have done most of what I set out to do, but find myself wondering each morning if there should not be more to life than running a pub. I hope that I am not becoming bored with my life simply because I seem to have met the challenge of making the Leo a busy and happy pub. Our holiday in Normandy is at the end of this month, and I am looking forward to waking up somewhere else each morning. Till then, I shall do my best to sparkle every session, keep my customers happy and play my proper part in our small community.

Saturday 3rd

I must stop feeling sorry for myself. Two new visitors have adopted us as their local, and have made me realise just how lucky I am to have a thriving business and all my faculties in reasonable working order. The young men work at the local Deaf Association where they teach sign language, and have begun to call in each evening.

They are unfailingly cheerful and polite, and have the courage and character to help others feel less uncomfortable about their disabilities by making light of them. Both are profoundly deaf, and it has been fascinating to learn the signing for a pint of lager and a packet of hedgehog crisps and how to have a basic conversation about the weather and how many goals our soccer team will lose by next weekend. We are firm friends now, but our first meeting started badly when one of them came up to the bar for a refill after I had rung the bell for closing time. Not knowing about his disability, I asked him if he was deaf, and reading my lips, he smiled and nodded and I wished I was somewhere else. The next evening, he presented me with a framed drawing of a ship's bell and suggested I hold it up when calling time so that he would not make the same mistake again. A little later, I saw the two friends standing at the bar, waving their glasses and opening and shutting their mouths in unison. When I hurried to serve them, he wrote something on a piece of paper and handed it to me with an impish grin. The message said that they were not waiting to be served, but having a singsong after a few drinks.

It is a very old pub gag, but coming from them and after my own petty grumbles, it made my heart sing for the heights the human spirit can sometimes attain.

Monday 5th

After nine months, we are to stage our first wedding reception. The couple are not regulars, but the best man phoned this afternoon to say he had been let down by their local pub and the situation was desperate. All they needed was a few sandwiches and a corner to celebrate the occasion with a small number of friends and family. I said I was sure that the Ship Leopard could do better than a selection of unimaginative sandwiches and pieces of bland cheese on cocktail sticks. We do not have a function room, but it will be easy to set up a buffet in the lounge bar and put up some extra decorations to create a special party atmosphere. I will engage Lamp Post Alec to put on an artful spread, and Deaf Dolly will provide the entertainment with a piano singalong.

I am slightly concerned that my wife and I will be on holiday on the big day, but Barry is sure he and the rest of the staff can cope. He has promised me that it will be an old-fashioned pub wedding knees-up, and one that the couple and their guests will remember for the rest of their lives together.

Thursday 8th

I have struck a blow for my profession by starting a pub bore competition. The idea came to me this evening after I had to listen to the same joke for the third time in the same session. What made it worse was that, like pub singers, compulsive joke-tellers invariably have no talent for timing and delivery. Another problem is that customers can escape to another pub or at least move along the bar when the resident bore appears. The publican has no choice but to either put up with it, invent an emergency in the cellar, or, in extreme cases, feign a heart attack. In my time at the Leo, I have endured endless hours of listening to involved stories about every non-subject from faulty central heating systems to the best way to remove caraway seeds from dentures.

Now, I am striking back with a nomination box on the counter and posters inviting entries for the Ship Leopard Bore of the Year Contest. First prize will be a weekend in Belgium for the winner, and the runner-up will also go so that the happy couple will be able to keep each other entertained. The competition has caught on, and a sneak preview at closing time revealed that the front runners are a pensioner whose main topic of conversation is the timetable of the local bus company, and a vegetarian who is trying to form an appreciation society for Brussels sprouts. It will be most suitable if he wins the trip to Belgium. Unfortunately, there are seven nominations for me in the box, but I shall remove them before judgement day.

Sunday 11th

A full house in spite of dreadful weather, and another true

eccentric has become a regular at the Club Leo. The Brigadier is an elderly gentleman of obvious military bearing who has taken to visiting us at all hours, and often when we are not open for business. He is very formal, obviously thinks I am his batman, and insists on personally measuring out the angostura bitters for his pink gin to ensure that the doseage is precisely right. I noticed on his first visit that he was wearing a set of old-fashioned striped pyjamas beneath his camel-hair topcoat, and he is under the impression he can sign for his drinks rather than pay for them. This morning I discovered that he believes the Ship Leopard is the committee room of the local Conservative club where he was honorary chairman for many years before it closed down through lack of support. I have appointed Barry as the Brigadier's minder, and he will see that he gets home safely every day and that he is comfortable in his sheltered accommodation apartment. How old people are treated is a measure of any society, and keeping an eye on the more vulnerable members of our neighbourhood is part of any self-respecting corner pub's responsibility.

Saturday 17th

The regulars have had their revenge for my pub bore competition. I have received a call from a Sunday newspaper to tell me I have been acclaimed The Worst Landlord in Britain. The reporter said the paper had received thousands of entries for other licensees across the country, but I had romped home by a ratio of fifteen to one votes more than my nearest rival. My alleged qualifications include boring the regulars with my bad jokes, my general stinginess, a lust for crazy stunts and self-publicity, extreme cruelty to the staff and customers, and my refusal to spend more than five minutes behind the bar. A photographer is arriving tomorrow to picture me together with the regulars who sent in the nominations, and there will be a story in the paper and a framed certificate to go on the wall. What my disloyal customers do not know is that the *News of the World* is also donating a barrel of free beer for those of my regulars who voted for me, and I shall take great delight in selling it to them by the glass.

Monday 19th

An article in the weekly trade journal has claimed there are moves to ban smoking in all public places, including public houses. The report said that the majority of customers do not like being in smokey pubs, and that non-smoking pubs are gaining in popularity. Staff are also said to be concerned about the danger to their health of being exposed to the deadly fumes for hours at a time.

I do not believe for a moment that only one third of adults smoke nowadays, as virtually all of my customers do, and it is hard enough to persuade my staff not to light up while they are actually serving drinks. Out of idle curiosity, I once counted the stubs in all our ashtrays after a busy session, and the total worked out at nearly a packet for every customer we had served. Pubs and smoking have always gone together, and nicotine has become part of the décor and general ambience. Our ceilings are a fetching shade of old gold as a result of the millions of cigarettes which have been smoked on the premises since they were last painted white, and there is something homely and almost comforting about the smell of stale smoke, beer and bodies which greets me as I come down the stairs each morning. I also know of at least one pub in the city that banned smoking with disastrous effect on takings. The licensee lost so much trade in a week that he had to scrap the rule, and the experience proved so stressful that he took up smoking.

I must think about the publicity value of declaring the Leopard a smokers-only pub for a week. It would be compulsory for all customers to light up within five minutes of arriving, and we could have happy hours with discounts on the leading brands of cigarettes, and cheap beer for anyone with two fags on the go at the same time. Anyone not smoking would be actively harrassed by other customers, or made to stand outside in the bottle yard to indulge his or her filthy non-habit.

Another furore in the press about the price of pub drinks. The story is a hardy perennial for the daily papers, and an ideal chance for sub-editors to whip themselves and their readers into a froth of righteous indignation while trotting out unimaginative headline puns about 'calling time' on profiteering landlords. As usual, all the reports are hopelessly inaccurate and show that nobody outside the trade understands anything about the business or, indeed, running any business. Like all salary-earning people, the reporters think that selling something for up to three times what you pay for it is worse than usury, and that trying to make a profit is nothing short of sharp practice. All I know is that my wife and I earn less than ten pounds an hour between us after paying all the expenses, and the Leopard is a lot busier than most other pubs in the city. A supermarket can turn over more money in a few minutes than the average pub takes in a week, and can afford to stack the goods high and sell them cheap. That's why the corner shop disappeared, and the same people who are whining about the price of a pint will be the first to complain when the traditional corner local goes the same way.

Tuesday 20th

We are off on our French leave tomorrow, and like a prisoner nearing the end of a long stretch, I am suffering from gate fever. The break will not only be a chance to relax and think about our long-term plans, but also to investigate a few typical French bars. All the surveys show that foreign visitors put a visit to a British pub at the top of their list of priorities when they visit this country, so it will be interesting to see where their local licensees are going wrong.

Wednesday 21st

It is raining in Normandy, and it is all very French. Apart from the weather, we might as well be on the other side of the world rather than just across the Channel, and our European neighbours seem to have a completely different way of doing things and looking at life. I have not yet found a bar with any customers remotely resembling my regulars, but my wife says this is hardly surprising, given that there is hopefully not another pub like the Ship Leopard in the whole of Britain.

My wife is enjoying herself immensely after making me promise not to talk about the Leo or what she calls the inmates, and we are staying in a small hotel in a fishing village on the west coast of the Cherbourg peninsula. The food is as good as the accommodation is indifferent, and I am told by other experienced guests that that is par for the course in the French hospitality industry. But I am sorely missing a decent pub with something going on to amuse the locals. I have reminded the bar manager at our hotel of the date and suggested he might want to liven the place up with a Trafalgar Day promotion, but he does not seem keen on the idea.

Friday 23rd

We are having a pleasant enough time, but I am still missing my home comforts. There are no British newspapers on sale, French TV is terrible, and I am told there is not a single curry house or fish and chip shop in the whole of this part of Normandy. My wife says that I am being a little Englander and should enjoy the differences rather than complain about them, but she is missing the point. There are at least a dozen French-style restuarants, wine and café bars within a mile of the Ship Leopard, so surely it is the French who are being chauvinistic and unadventurous by not trying traditional English cuisine and entertainments?

I can also see why foreigners think so much of our pubs, as the bars on offer here are as exciting as a doctor's waiting room. Last night we went on a pub crawl in Cherbourg, and in spite of it being a big town, the bars we visited were virtually empty. The nearest equivalent of the local is a cheaply converted shop with tiled floor, plastic chairs and tables and a handful of bored-looking people nursing a glass of beer. The choice is limited to lager, lager or lager, and the people behind the bar make my staff look like cabaret stars. Even if I could speak French, the potential for a philosophical conversation about life appears non-existent, and all one hears is the odd grunt which reminds me of the previous landlord at the Leopard.

To be fair, one can see why the licensees of all these little bars look so miserable. For a race which is said to have the highest alcohol consumption rate in Europe, French people obviously do all their serious drinking at home. There is no such thing as a pint glass even though they invented the measure, and some customers actually take their beer in a tiny wine glass, then sit looking glumly at it for hours while it evaporates. The customers and staff seem astonished at my consumption rate, especially when I order two glasses at a time to avoid negotiating for a refill every ten minutes. It is also unnerving to see so many children on licenced premises, instead of being properly shut away in a family room or left in good hands at home, and the lack of any bar food is disgraceful. We are constantly lectured about our catering shortcomings by the sort of chattering-class idiots who seem to think that French equals good and English bad in all matters, but I have not been to a single bar which offers a packet of crisps or pork scratchings, let alone a simple jar of pickled eggs or onions on the bar. The range of pub grub is limited to a ham or cheese roll if you ask nicely, and then the owner has to send out to the nearest baker's shop for the bread. I have suggested to my wife that we should look seriously at the idea of opening a real British pub in Cherbourg to show the locals what they are missing, but she will not even discuss the idea.

If the bars have not come up to my expectations, however, the price and availability of property is a revelation. The French do not generally seem to value or care much about their homes, and DIY stores are as rare as a friendly policeman. Driving in the countryside we have come across dozens of dilapidated cottages and defunct farmhouses, and the prices are astonishingly low when compared to England. My wife has reminded me of my promise to buy her a home in the country, and she seems quite content that it be in a foreign country. She has already visited a dozen estate agents and collected details of hundreds of properties in need of restoration. Most lack such basic niceties as a roof, but the average price would not buy a garage in the Hampshire countryside.

After several glasses of apple brandy this evening, my wife suggested that we buy a derelict farmhouse before we leave, then she will come back and restore it while I run the Ship Leopard and send regular money orders over to pay for the work. I would be allowed to visit her every other weekend, and after a few more years at the Leo, I could sell the lease of the pub and join her for an early retirement in our country home. I promised to think about the idea, but suggested she might be lonely in the middle of nowhere with just a cement mixer for company and without me or any of our friends and customers at the Leo to talk to.

After another glass of local firewater, she said that she would be perfectly happy with her dog, cat and menagerie, and would anyway find the company and conversation of a cement mixer much more stimulating than the regulars at the Ship bloody Leopard. The evening ended with a row, but I'm sure that by the morning she will have forgotten what she said and, hopefully, her plans for deserting me.

Saturday 24th

The car is loaded down to its axles with my wife's lists of French property and more than a dozen cases of wine for my personal consumption. Surprisingly, I have developed a taste for French wine in the past week, and I have to admit it is a drink they do well. As with property, the prices are almost risible compared with what one would have to pay at home. In the big supermarket on the hill outside Cherbourg, trays of beer and every type of wine and spirits can be bought at less than the price I can buy them wholesale in England, but after my experiences with the Customs and Excise Gestapo, I have not been tempted to buy any stock for the Leo. My wine collection will be safely locked away in my private cupboard in the bottle store, and anyway, they would be of little interest to my customers. Sales of wine at the Leo are limited to one case of German sweet white a fortnight, and the bag of red plonk connected to a tap on the bar has not been changed since I took over last January.

Sunday 25th, 8 am:

Dreadful news from home. Deaf Dolly has been on the phone to say that the Ship Leopard has been destroyed and Dirty Barry is in prison. Despite shouting at the top of my voice I could get no further sense from her, so we must pack up and return on the next ferry.

Home Brew

Wine grew in popularity in Britain from 1066, but for many hundreds of years before the Conquest it was invariably ale or nothing. As Pliny the Elder recorded with grudging admiration:

'The natives who inhabit the west of Europe have a liquid with which they intoxicate themselves made from corn and water. So exquisite is the cunning of mankind in gratifying their vicious appetites that they have thus invented a method to make water itself produce intoxication...'

NOVEMBER

Thankfully, the situation is not as bad as Dolly said. But it is bad enough, and the inside of the Ship Leopard has been devastated.

All the mirrors behind the bar have been smashed, the windows shattered, and the beer pumps torn from the counter top. Light fittings have been ripped from the ceiling and walls, most of the chairs and tables have been broken, and the carpet is soaked in blood and vomit. Even the legs of Old Joe's armchair were snapped off for use as weapons by our rioting guests.

It seems the wedding party ran amok in both bars shortly after the best man tried to bring his horse into the bar. The couple are descended from travellers and arrived in traditional manner in a gypsy cart. Obviously, they also decided to end the wedding feast in an equally traditional manner by having a good punch-up between the two families. According to the surviving eye-witnesses, the trouble started when the mother of the bride had words with the groom about some delicate breach of etiquette on her daughter's special day. He compared her unfavourably with his horse, and his new wife turned on him with the knife they had just used to cut the cake Lamp Post Alec had so lovingly created. The attempted decapitation of the groom was the signal for a general outbreak of violence between the two families, and the arrival of the police made matters worse, with the opposing sides uniting to take on the mutual enemy. The climax came when the heavily pregnant bride head-butted a policewoman who was trying to calm her down, and, still in her dress of virginal white, she was carted off with her husband and their guests to spend their first honeymoon night in separate cells. According to Mandy Melons, Dirty Barry was set upon by the groom's grandmother as he tried to restore order, and was taken into custody when the woman accused him of attacking her. The old crone's parting shot was to lay the second dread curse on the Ship Leopard this year, and my reporter friend Skint Eastwood has betrayed me by circulating the story to the media. The front page of the local paper has a banner headline about the fight and the curse, and a photograph showing the bride defiantly throwing her bouquet to the spectators as she is wrestled in to the police van.

For once, I can see that not all publicity is good publicity. The physical damage is repairable, but nearly a year of all our efforts to build the reputation of the Leo as a respectable and friendly pub may have been wiped out in a single afternoon.

Monday 2nd

After a mostly sleepless night, I came down this morning and stood amongst the wreckage of our little pub. Tez the Prez says that you can tell a lot about a public house and its trade and licensee just by visiting the premises during closing time. The real clues are not whether the carpet sticks to your feet, the décor and type of drinks on sale or even if there are teeth marks on the furniture. He is an immensely practical man, but believes that long years of trading actually charges the atomosphere of any pub with the spirit of its host and his customers. A pub which has been a generally happy meeting place will have a quiet and contented atmosphere after closing time. Where violence and unhappiness have been regular customers, they will have left their unmistakable echoes in the very air. I know it is only a pub, but after our countless hours of striving to make it a friendly and welcoming place for decent people to come and relax, I feel the Leo has been violated.

*   *   *   *   *

Tez has called with some more information about the gypsy families who wrecked the Leo. He says the engaged couple were desperate for somewhere to hold their reception because they and their relatives are barred from nearly every pub in the city. For obvious reasons, the best man gave me a false name when he made the booking. Even the Black Dog turned them down though they are regulars there, and Tez says he has heard on the pub grapevine that Casser Blygh suggested they try the Ship Leopard. He knew what would be the inevitable outcome of the two tribes coming together, and it has become a running joke along the strip that he helped me wreck my own pub.

After our conversation, I sat in the cellar for a long while, then made a couple of phone calls. The landlord of the Black Dog may think he has had the last laugh, but now the gloves are off, and it is time for me to respond in kind.

Wednesday 4th

During World War II, the city's naval base and ancient dockyard was a prime target for the German airforce, and it is still a source of local pride that the continuous and ferocious bombing campaigns could not break the spirit of the citizens and army of city traders. I have adopted this defiant attitude, and put up a sign advertising business as usual, but it is hard to maintain a brave face.

The worst part is the spectators who come to gawp mindlessly as if at the scene of a road accident, and the sniggers and mock sympathy from some of my competitors when they arrive to gloat over the damage to my pub and its reputation. One consolation is that my regulars have been supportive and are clearly outraged by the attack on the Leo; another is that takings are up from the increased throughput of rubberneckers.

Tuesday 17th

The restoration work is now complete, and I have taken the opportunity to reverse some of the structural amendments made in my early months at the Leo. The partition between the two bars has reappeared, and the carpet in the public bar has been replaced with the modern equivalent of linoleum. The manufacturers advertise their toughest variety of floorcovering with a picture of a tank rolling over it, so it should hopefully withstand the attentions of my pool and darts teams. The original etched windows the wedding party smashed were irreplaceable, but I have made a feature of the new ones. Using reverse marketing and to cock a snook at the area's real ale bores, the advertising blurbs on the glass now tell passers-by that our beer is terrible, and the food and service even worse.

As an added gimmick, I persuaded the signwriter to misspell the list of our products, and at least a dozen new customers have come in to point out that the sign should read 'lager', not 'larger'. I've also taken the opportunity to have a special door built for the Gents toilet, which now looks like the entrance to a nuclear bunker. With a metal plate covering each side and double the normal number of hinges, the door took three very strong men to lift in to place, and the foreman assures me it would take an explosive charge laid by an expert safecracker to get it off again.

This evening we staged an informal ceremony to mark the completion of the work, with Old Joe cutting a ribbon across the new old armchair I have bought him. As closing time approached I saw him looking around with quiet amusement, and asked what he thought of the new Leo. He gave a wry grunt, supped at his beer, then observed dryly that I have spent a lot of money changing the place back to exactly what it was like when I arrived.

Friday 20th

I have been dropped from my starring role on television. An embarrassed producer took me to one side when we had finished the latest episode to point out that, rather than losing weight as the series progressed, I have actually put on another stone, so they are going to have to abandon the series. I affected bitter disappointment, but to be honest, I am glad to be off the hook. Now I can eat and drink what I like, and concentrate on the build-up to Christmas. A bizarre incident in our bedroom should also make any publicity gained from my regional TV appearances seem small beer indeed.

Having gone upstairs a little after midnight last Saturday evening after a heavy session, I undressed, threw myself gratefully down on the bed and set off a chain reaction. As I landed beside my wife and Tyson, there was a groaning crash, and the bed legs were driven through the frail 19th-century floorboards. As a result, lumps of plaster cascaded down from the ceiling of the public bar and triggered the burglar alarm I had installed during the recent renovation work.

While the lights outside the pub flashed and sirens screamed, the police arrived to find me in my underwear behind the bar, consoling myself and our neighbours with a calming nightcap. Next morning, I casually mentioned the incident to Skint Eastwood, and his tabloid nose immediately began to twitch. Though I could not see the news value in such a trivial event, he was on the phone to his London press contacts within the hour, and our world has gone mad. After all the stunts I have contrived to win free advertising for the Ship Leopard, the media reaction and scale of response to the true story of the bed-breaking incident has taken me completely by surprise. The telephone has not stopped ringing since my spin doctor dressed up the details of how the outsize landlord of the Leo broke his bed during a Naughty Night Of Nookie, and the press have gone into a feeding frenzy.

Monday 23rd

The bed story has taken on a life of its own as the worldwide media compete to give the basic facts a fresh twist. Skint Eastwood is making a fortune in fees, and has appointed himself as my full-time manager and agent. To make the story more visually appealing, he insists that I dress up in a ridiculous nightgown and cap when being interviewed, and he has even provided a focal point in the pub for the horde of cameramen arriving each day. A set of bed legs from the junk shop over the road has been fixed permanently to the ceiling of the public bar, and pilgrims are pouring in from all over the city to marvel at the sight.

Based on the incredible level of publicity, my manager has also secured me a contract with the world's biggest bed maker. According to their PR department, the manufacturers have a robot which replicates the actions of a sleeping man and helps them to design their beds to withstand maximum stress. Now, I am to become the firm's first-ever human bed tester, and there are even plans for me to replace the hippopotamus which normally stars in their television commercials. I am also booked to appear on a TV panel game where the celebrity contestants will have to guess my profession, and then there will be a nationwide tour of bedding shops, when I will once again be working with Twiggy Bristols. The proposed routine is to set a stepladder up in the window, then I will climb to the top in my Wee Willie Winkie nightgown before throwing myself on to one of the sponsoring company's indestructible beds. My wife has naturally refused to have anything to do with these antics, and Twiggy's role is to dress in a skimpy French maid's outfit and lay on the bed for no other reason than to provide an even more appealing picture for the press.

I don't know how long my instant celebrity will last, but I am enjoying myself immensely, and the publicity is doing wonders for trade at the Leo.

*   *   *   *   *

My agent has been in to show me the latest press cuttings from around the world, and I shall never again believe a single word I read in any newspaper. Outrageously dressed-up stories have appeared in leading journals in America, New Zealand, Australia and any number of other English-speaking countries. I have not yet appeared on the cover of *Time* magazine, but it can only be a matter of time. I could not make out what the foreign language publications have been saying about me and my alleged activities, but the photographs of me descending on Twiggy Bristols from a great height have obviously captured the imagination of editors and readers across the planet.

As most pub regulars make the frantic last-minute bid to save for Christmas, times are hard for my colleagues along the strip, but the Ship Leopard is full. The sharp winter winds buffet against our doors and blow the crowds in to stare in wonder at the fake bed legs screwed into the public bar ceiling, and I and the Leo are becoming famous just for being famous. Simply because of the nature of the story, the public also seems to think that I am an expert on everything to do with beds, and everything that goes on in them. Yesterday I received an invitation from a London radio station to host a phone-in about listeners' sexual problems, and an American soft-porn TV channel has enquired if I would like to make a video with their leading starlet. I have become particularly celebrated in the United States as a result of a taped interview my agent syndicated to more than five hundred radio stations, and their disc jockeys have taken to calling me at all hours for live interviews.

Knowing what their audiences want to hear and their general level of credulity, Skint Eastwood has coached me in a routine which includes claiming that I am sitting in the bar looking out at Nelson's flagship *Victory*, and that Charles Dickens, Shakespeare, Margaret Thatcher and Sherlock Holmes are amongst my regular customers. After making sure I mention the name of my bed company sponsors at least twice, I then oblige my interviewer by taking part in a live on-air testing session. Following a dramatic countdown, I pretend to launch myself from the top of my wardrobe while Skint Eastwood mans the sound effects equipment and twangs an old bedspring to simulate splashdown.

Another unexpected outcome from my newsworthiness is that I now have an academic degree. When I left school with no formal qualifications, I drifted through a series of dead-end jobs and always regretted not having sat for a single examination when I had the chance. After working in the mindless hell of a cardboard box-making factory for a year, I fell in with a group of left-wing college lecturers who believed that the only qualification for gaining a university education should be the desire to do so, and they set about using me as a test case.

With their help, I spent my evenings studying for and apparently gaining a handful of basic education certificates, and was eventually admitted to a Polytechnic degree course in English. It was one of the most challenging and rewarding times of my life, but my further education lasted less than a term before I was hauled before the education board and asked to explain why I had submitted forged certificates. Walking back through the gates of the cardboard box factory to re-start my sentence was the only time in my life that I have felt remotely like killing myself.

Now and after all these years, I at last have letters after my name. I learned yesterday that I have been awarded a Doctorate in Bedology by a correspondence college in Nebraska. I shall enjoy using the title when it suits me, but it is not really the same as having earned a proper degree from a more universally recognised educational establishment.

Thursday 26th

We have marked the approach of the festive season by taking the permanent Christmas decorations down and ceremonially putting them up again. My agent is now talking about taking our old bed on a worldwide lecture tour, but I think it will come to nothing. My taste of stardom has been an interesting experience, but I know that a fleeting kiss from dame celebrity is no indication of a lasting union. It has been the strangest period of my apprenticeship at the Leo, which is saying something. Now, my first year behind bars is coming to an end, and I have mixed feelings about what I have achieved and where I want to be this time next year. For the moment, it is time to get ready for Christmas and to coolly plot and take my revenge on Casser Blygh.

Simply The Best

Regardless of the passing fads and fashions in the licensed profession, the last word on the eternal value and appeal of our national institution should be left to that great man of letters, Doctor Samuel Johnson, who said:

'There is no private house in which people can enjoy themselves as well as at a capital tavern. At a tavern, there is a general freedom of anxiety...(and) you are sure to be welcome. No sir, there is nothing which has yet been conceived by man by which so much happiness is produced as by a good tavern or inn...'

DECEMBER

The countdown to our first Christmas behind bars has begun, and today we laid in more than enough provisions to withstand the coming siege. Our huge stock of extra spirits has been stowed in the cellar below the floorboards of the bar area, and a small mountain of extra crates and kegs are stacked in the bottle yard store. As Barry and I rested from our labours this lunchtime, Flash Gordon the pub inspector made his daily appearance, and it was time to put my plans in action. Taking him on a guided tour and ignoring my manager's puzzled looks, I made a point of telling Gordon just how many thousands of pounds worth of valuable spirits are now housed in the bottle yard store, how flimsy the padlock on the door is, and how our new and erratic burglar alarm is on the blink again.

Friday 4th

Peter the Pipes arrived early this morning for our unofficial and very private appointment. After explaining my need for his expert help, I led the way into the bottle store, leaving strict instructions that we were not to be disturbed for any emergencies short of a return visit from the gypsy wedding party.

Saturday 5th

A very nervous Barry called up the stairs this morning to say that Charlie the Demon Barber had arrived in the public bar, and was asking to see me. Even I felt a frisson of nervousness at the news, though it was I who had summoned him from his dark and dangerous world.

Despite his pub name, Charlie has never been a member of

the hairdressing fraternity, but earned his grisly sobriquet and reputation from his penchant for carrying a pair of pearl-handled cutthroat razors in his younger days. I don't know how many of the grim stories of how he carved out a successful career in the city's underworld are true, but I am glad he is an old acquaintance, and happier still that he does not use the Leo as his local. Although his range of illicit interests and nefarious activities is wide, Charlies' main line of business at this time of year is taking orders for and supplying a wide range of goods at well below wholesale prices. His official line is that he can provide such bargains as he is selling direct and bypassing the normal supply chain. As I know that most of the goods he supplies come direct from their rightful owners and how he ensures no comeback, this puts a whole new slant on the idea of cutting out the middle man. After I had explained my propositions, the Demon Barber went happily about his unlawful business, but is obviously bemused at our unusual arrangement.

Monday 7th

El Sid has been in with the news that his team is being split up, so the Leo will no longer be the unofficial headquarters for the city's Criminal Investigation Department. Apparently, news that the squad has been spending more time on duty at my pub than out on the mean streets of the city has got back to a busybody superior, and Sid and his colleagues are to be dispersed to other stations around the county. As he said, now that the Leo is known to be such a respectable tavern, the excuse that they had been spending so much time on the premises to keep an eye on the local villainry was a non-starter. In a moving ceremony, Sid and his colleagues then presented me with a pair of specially engraved handcuffs as a reminder of our many enjoyable lock-ins, and assured me that the full team will be on duty at the Leo for the Christmas period.

I shall be sorry to lose them, but always knew their departure would be inevitable. Since my arrival at the Leo, I have come to understand that part of the sweet sadness of running a pub is the natural ebb and flow of customers, and that losing a cherished regular can be like losing a good friend. Especially when that customer is a really good spender.

Sunday 13th

We have been burgled. After another blissful night on our free king-sized bed, I went downstairs to find the yard gates had been expertly jemmied open, and the door to the bottle store wrenched off its hinges. My newly-arrived Christmas stock of spirits and tubs is still safe in the cellar below the public bar, and El Sid says the thieves obviously decided to settle for the six kegs of lager in the overflow store. Barry is outraged at the break-in, and puzzled by my apparent lack of concern at our loss. He also cannot understand why the burglars would go to so much trouble to steal a few barrels of beer which can only be used with the proper dispensing equipment. I have explained that we are covered by insurance, that the stolen tubs are virtually untraceable, and would doubtless find a ready market with an unscrupulous licensee in search of a bargain buy at this busy time of year.

Wednesday 16th

Not a good start to my day when I found my private collection of fine French wines has been ransacked. A particular blow was to find three bottles of especially expensive vintage missing. Rooting around in the skip I found the empty bottles, and Barry has confessed that he and not our burglars is the culprit. He said that he had run out of our normal supplies of cheap red wine during the ladies dart match last night, and in my absence had used his initiative. The visiting team had complained about the taste and overall quality of my private collection from the finest *chateaux* in all France, but he had mollified them by charging half the price of the usual stuff which comes out of the pump on the bar.

Thursday 17th

El Sid returned this morning to tell me that his team has had no luck in finding our burglars. He also took the opportunity to arrest one of my most valuable new public bar customers. Introducing himself as Dusty, the small and inoffensive man has spent the last week getting quietly pickled every afternoon and paying his bill with the contents of a collection of envelopes. He wears bright orange overalls and gives off a bouquet of rotting vegetables, so I had naturally assumed he was a dustman. After feeling his collar and before escorting him to the station, Sid explained that his captive is actually an enterprising huckster who regularly spends the week before Christmas visiting homes just before the dustcart arrives to wish the householders the season's greetings and pick up any tips. Yesterday he made the mistake of calling on the house of one of the official refuse collectors for the area, and has been taken into custody for his own protection while the charges are being sorted out.

Saturday 19th

The saddest of news this morning. Old Joe did not appear at his regular time, and his taxi driver arrived an hour later with only Nosher the dog as his passenger. The driver told us that our longest-serving regular passed peacefully away in his sleep last night. It is strange to think that Old Joe will never again come stumping through the door to keep us all on our toes.

*　　*　　*　　*　　*

We held Joe's wake this evening, and I was surprised and touched to see how many people turned up to show their respect for our oldest regular. Joe Brinningham had no living relatives, but many former comrades and drinking partners from the British Legion put in an appearance, and three unhappy licensees arrived to say that he had also been a regular at their pubs. It was a dignified occasion, and I was glad I did not take up Barry's suggestion that we ask the undertakers to prop up the corpse of our most regular old regular in his chair so that he could enjoy a last session at his favourite local. At closing time, Barry asked if I would like him to get rid of Joe's armchair, but I said it will stay as long as I am licensee at the Leo.

After everyone had gone, I sat thinking about him and how strange it was that we would never see our curmudgeonly old soldier again, and that the Leo will certainly not be the same without him. He did not suffer fools gladly, had a waspish tongue and macabre sense of humour, but came from a different time and world, and was old enough to say what he really thought. His type are literally a dying breed, and it is wrong to judge them by today's standards. After I put the lights out and hung Joe's tankard up for the last time, it took me a while to persuade Nosher to leave his master's chair and follow me up the stairs to his new home. Like Joe, he has been part of our lives for almost a year, and it is somehow fitting that he will stay with us. Besides, he will make a far more effective guard dog than Tyson.

Tuesday 22nd

The Ship Leopard Christmas Club payout takes place this evening, and the day has already not been without drama.

Flash Gordon the pub inspector arrived breathlessly this morning to say that Casser Blygh is in big trouble. The strip is afire with the word that the Black Dog was raided early this morning and the licensee arrested. Later in the day, El Sid came in with the details, and said my arch-rival has been charged with a number of offences, including watering his beer. After a complaint by an anonymous customer, the Dog was visited this morning by a combined team of police and Customs and Excise officials.

Acting on information received, they found a number of barrels of lager in his cellar which had been tampered with. Not only was the licensee unable to show delivery notes for the watered beer, but also and much more importantly, the investigators found a hoard of other illicit drinks and cigarettes on which Casser Blygh had obviously avoided duty.

Other incriminating items were found in the private quarters upstairs, and it looks as if the licensee of the Black Dog has been doubling as a receiver of stolen goods as well as a notorious landlord. Now, the Inland Revenue will be going through his accounts for the last ten years at least, and he will not wriggle off the hook. Casser Blygh is sure to lose his licence as a fit and proper landlord, and more than probably his liberty. It is a particularly satisfactory end to El Sid's tour of duty in this area as he has been after Blygh for years. From his point of view, the strangest aspect of the affair is that the landlord of the Black Dog should be so stupid as to water his beer and give the Excise men a chance to go into action.

I bought my friend a drink and muttered a few words about the folly of greed, and made a mental note to make a special fuss of Pete the Pipes and Charlie the Demon Barber when they arrive for the payout party this evening.

*　　*　　*　　*　　*

Midnight:

The party is in full swing, and I am sitting in my special corner of the lounge bar with my wife and Nosher alongside. Tyson has predictably accepted that there is a new top dog in the household, and is quietly sleeping away his hangover in the bottle store.

Both bars are packed to more than capacity, the cash register is genuinely approaching meltdown, and nearly everyone who has contributed to our first year at the Ship Leopard Tavern has been in to wish us well and tell us their news. Twiggy Bristols has returned to make a special celebrity appearance behind the bar, and she and Mandy Melons are having to use my lay-by to pass each other. Our former star barmaid has told me that she is now a movie star, though her first film is only available on video from a special address, but she is sending me a copy for the regulars to remember her by.

Elsewhere, Barry is proudly wearing the special manager's waistcoat my wife knitted for him, and Deaf Dolly is serving a bewildered customer with fourteen packets of hedgehog crisps. An unlikely romance has blossomed between Desperate Anne and Graham the transvestite gravedigger, and they are excitedly discussing the possibilities of the extended wardrobes their new relationship brings.

On the pool table, Spare Parts Paddy and Long Molly are taking on allcomers, and Wingco and Lamp Post Alec are competing with Mr Woolworths to win a special nomination for the latest Fall of the Month trophy. By the juke box, Mad Max the shady dealer is trying to sell his surplus crystal balls to El Sid and the CID boys, and Skint Eastwood is leaning against the fruit machine, dreaming of his next big scoop. In a nearby corner, The Red Baron is exchanging wartime memories with the Brigadier, and Still Standing Albert is swaying comfortably from his handbag hook. Goodwill abounds, and even the Brothers Grim are smiling at each other.

As the party gathers momentum, I find myself thinking about my year behind bars, and what I have learned in my attempt to create the perfect corner pub. I came to change the Ship Leopard; instead, and as Old Joe said so wisely, the pub and the people here have changed me. Perhaps I have learned to be a little more tolerant of others; I have certainly learned more about how other people lead their lives. Most importantly of all, I think I have discovered that the secret of a good pub is that there is no secret. Part of what makes the magic is the right landlord in the right pub, and the rich mix of people who use it. As anyone who has searched long and hard for his perfect pub will tell you, there must also be some indefinable quality that can only be achieved by time, careful nurture and happy chance.

Of one thing I'm sure. The British pub is a part of our nation's culture and identity, and it will be a true tragedy if we should ever lose what it represents and says about us. For me, it has been a time of small adventures and a switchback ride of moods ranging through fear, frustration and anger to sadness, elation and quiet contentment. It has also been an experience I shall remember all my life. I don't know if we shall all be here this time next year, but whatever lies ahead, I know that my year behind bars has taught me much more than it has cost.

For now, cheers.

The Ultimate Pub Quiz

If, despite having read this book you like the idea of running your own pub, this carefully devised but simple test could reveal whether your character, personality and attitude are generally suited to a life behind bars. All you have to do is choose the answers with which you agree, tot up your score, then check your personal 'pubability' rating.

Question 1

Do you like to take a drink?

a) Occasionally

b) Never

c) Often

d) Do bears pooh in the woods?

Question 2

Do you and your partner enjoy each other's company?

a) Most of the time

b) Some of the time

c) Rarely

d) I'll ask him/her when we're speaking again

Question 3

Are you good with money?

a) Give me a tenner and I'll tell you

b) Yes

c) No

d) When I've got some

Question 4

Do you like people?

a) On the whole, yes
b) If I make the effort
c) No
b) As long as they don't keep asking me stupid questions like these

Question 5

Are you a hard worker?

a) Yes
b) When I need to
c) Not if I can avoid it
d) I can't be bothered to finish this quiz

Question 6

Are you a good listener?

a) Yes
b) I try to be
c) I'd rather do the talking
d) What was the question?

Question 7

Are you a tolerant person?

a) I try to be
b) I think so
c) Not always
d) What a stupid question - of course I am

Question 8

Can you be diplomatic?

a) That's an interesting question
b) When it's necessary
c) If I feel like it
d) This is the same question as before, you moron

Question 9

Do you handle potentially nasty incidents well?

a) I'm a trained hostage negotiator
b) I've got a black belt in Karate
c) Don't know, I always walk away from them
d) Come outside and I'll show you, pinhead

Question 10

Could you manage employees well?

a) I like to think I'd be firm but fair
b) If they do exactly what they're told
c) I'd leave that sort of thing to my partner
d) I'd be so popular, people would work for me for nothing

Question 11

Would you really like to be your own boss?

a) I already am
b) I don't honestly know, but I'm ready to give it my best shot
c) I love the idea of being in charge
d) It has to be better than working for someone else

Question 12

Would you mind working while your customers are enjoying themselves?

a) As long as it's good for business, no
b) Of course not - it gives me pleasure to make other people happy
c) To be honest, yes
d) Running a pub is not like real work, you dummy

Question 13

Finally, what makes you think you'd be good at running a pub?

a) I like people and pubs
b) I like pubs and people
c) I spend most of my spare time in pubs
d) Any fool could do it, so why not me?

Scoring:

To assess your pubability rating, award yourself:

3 points for each (a) answer you chose
2 points for each (b) answer you chose
1 point for each (c) answer you chose
0 points for each (d) answer you chose

Ratings

39 points and over: At face value, it seems you could have what it takes to be a successful publican. Perhaps, though, you have not been totally honest about yourself (which is not necessarily a handicap in the industry) or don't really understand yourself or other people (ditto). If you have scored more than 39 points, you either cheated or are so bad at adding up you'll need to get someone else to keep a close eye on the finances. Mind you, an inclination towards over-estimation can be a real bonus when totting up a bar tab.

20–39 points: You are obviously practical, tolerant, businesslike, optimistic, adaptable and honest. Or like people to think you are. This could be a major advantage as a publican, but have you thought about going into politics instead?

0-20 points: You are clearly lacking many of the qualities of character, inter-personal skills, diplomacy, application and practicality necessary to make a success out of any career requiring these virtues. Perhaps you should think about becoming an estate agent, or even a lawyer?

0 points (and below): According to the panel of eminent psychologists who compiled this quiz, you are aggressive, intolerant, duplicitous, self-seeking and completely egocentric. Or you didn't bother to answer the questions. If you truly scored this badly and considering the behaviour and type of some of the customers licensees have to endure, perhaps a life behind bars might suit you very well.

GLOSSARY

This section attempts to explain the meaning of some of the more specialist, obscure or impenetrable words and references in *A Year Behind Bars*. Hopefully, it will be of use to overseas readers, infrequent pub-goers and those who have led a particularly sheltered life.

Brown Split: A drink which is also known for some obscure reason as a boilermaker, and is a mixture of mild beer and bottled brown ale. Not to be asked for in some rougher gay pubs.

Mickey Mouse: Revolting mixture of cider and bitter, favoured by stag parties and other people with little sense of taste who want to get very drunk very quickly.

Punters: Common trade term for customers (orig. English race course bookmakers' slang).

Headaches: Common trade term for awkward customers.

Arseholes: Common trade term for especially awkward customers.

Freehouse: Pub that is free of any tie to a brewery, so can sell any brand of drinks. Confusingly, a freehouse can also be a freehold (owned lock, stock and barrel by the licensee) or not.

Publican: The person who holds the licence for and physically manages any particular public house. Other common terms include licensee, landlord, guv'nor or miserable bastard.

Fags: Cigarettes. (Caution: if you are from another part of the English-speaking world, it is not advisable to go into an American bar and ask if they sell fags.)

Real Ale: All ale is 'real', but this is the common term for the traditional mixture of hops, yeast, barley, malt and water which leaves the brewery still alive and working in the barrel.

Keg: Generic term for beers like lager and bitter that have been specially treated (real ale bores would say 'killed') before leaving the brewery so the barrels can be tapped and served from immediately.

Arrows: The traditional pub game of darts, thought to have been invented by bored English archers during the Middle Ages, and now virtually the only sport invented in Britian at which we can still beat the rest of the world. Or most of it.

Slate: The original credit card, harking back to when pub regulars would have their personal tabs chalked up on a piece of slate kept behind the bar.

Boozer: Any rough pub, though sometimes a person using one. A public house may also be referred to as a local, a rub-a-dub (Cockney rhyming slang) or more formally as a hostelry, inn or tavern.

Local: Sometimes a favourite pub, sometimes the person who uses it.

Barney: Anything from a verbal altercation to full-blown fracas. Other pub terms for a fight include punch-up, scrap, set-to or bounce-up.

Squaddies: Soldiers.

Matelots/Skates: Sailors.

Round: Any selection of drinks bought by one person for his or (rarely) her drinking companions.

Pouffe: Common English slang expression for a homosexual. Also and sometimes confusingly, a soft foot-stool.

Skint: Broke, penniless.

Musical Feet: Reference to someone with a personal odour problem, and therefore whose feet are said to 'hum'.

Knee-trembler: Upright sexual intercourse, most usually al fresco.

The Mill of the Flea series

Home & Dry in France follows the early adventures of George and Donella East as the innocents abroad search for a home in France, discover The Little Jewel, and eventually arrive at the Mill of the Flea.

Home & Dry in France by George East ISBN: 0 9523635 0 X

The second book in the Mill of the Flea saga, *René & Me* charts a memorable year as our heroes attempt to survive with a series of bizarre and doomed schemes. As plans for staging metal-detecting weekends to unearth the miller's gold fall about their ears, René Ribet moves on to their land and in to their lives.
Also available as an audio book.

René & Me by George East ISBN: 0 9523635 1 8

In *French Letters*, the Easts continue their adventures in a land where time is cheap, good friends priceless, and reluctant tractors are brought to life on a frosty morning with a shot of moonshine brandy. During another eventful year at the Mill of the Flea, we meet a new host of improbable characters and events.

French Letters by George East ISBN: 0 9523635 2 6

The fourth book in the best-selling saga, *French Flea Bites* finds The Easts encountering new and increasingly bizarre characters and situations, including a man who believes he died in 1979, a cat who becomes a werewolf at full moon, and a plan by the Jolly Boys Club to turn the village compost heap into Néhou's answer to the Millennium Dome. As we join the Easts at the start of a new century, all is obviously *normale* at the Mill of the Flea…

French Flea Bites by George East ISBN: 0 9523635 3 4

"..Any new reader with a sense of humour and humanity will immediately enlist in the ever-growing army of George East's adoring fans."